# The Mouse with the Question Mark Tail

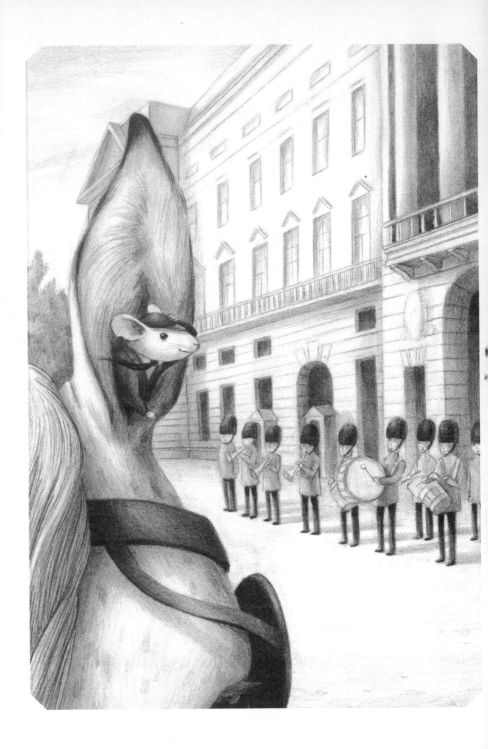

# The Mouse with the Question Mark Tail

A NOVEL BY

## Richard Peck

ILLUSTRATED BY

## Kelly Murphy

SCHOLASTIC INC.

ISBN 978-0-545-64797-7

12 11 10 9 8 7 6 5 4 3 2            13 14 15 16 17 18/0

Printed in the U.S.A.        23

First Scholastic printing, November 2013

Designed by Jennifer Kelly
Text set in Adobe Jenson

For
**Carl Pritzkat**
&
**Tony Travostino**

# Contents

# The Mouse with the Question Mark Tail

# A Royal Reminder

E VERY TIME A human walks out of a room, something with more feet walks in.

Mice, of course, who are only a whisker away and everywhere you fail to look. It's true of the room where you're sitting. It's truer still of Buckingham Palace.

How busy the scampering world of mice within the palace walls, through that mousehole just behind the throne. How busy the Royal Mews next door where the royal carriages are kept and the royal horses stabled. Beneath the clattering cobblestones of the Royal Mews a whole private honeycomb of mouse passages crisscross and connect. One of them leads into the palace itself.

How busy these royal places always are—

where you can see and where you are not allowed. And never busier than that distant June day when Queen Victoria celebrated her Diamond Jubilee: sixty years upon the throne!

Remember that great day when all the horses of the Royal Mews stamped across London in the proud jubilee parade. And the mice of Buckingham Palace swept out of the walls in a great gray tide that flowed across marble floors.

Remember that day, for it bears upon the story of my life.

# PART ONE

## The Royal Mews

CHAPTER ONE

# The Smallest Mouse in the Mews

W E WHO LIVED in the Royal Mews next door to Buckingham Palace—horses, humans, mice, one cat, a cow for the milk, and the occasional goat—were in the service of Her Majesty Queen Victoria, Queen of England and Empress of India.

The sun never sets on her empire, and there we were, right under her palace windows.

The Mews is a private world within four high walls that smells of horse and what horses leave behind. THE PUBLIC IS NOT ADMITTED, as the Mews is full of official secrets. And just possibly I was one of them.

I, the smallest mouse in the Mews, not grown nearly enough to match my ears or my eyes or my appetite. Always hungry as boys are, human or mouse.

And another thing about me. My tail. It was regular and standard-issue. Gray. About the right length for flailing. And naturally very useful for covering my tracks.

But there was something unusual about my tail. If I wasn't whipping it about or tucking it round me for the night or using it for balance as you do, it fell naturally into the shape of a question mark.

I was the mouse with the question mark tail. Perhaps because I was full of questions, many of them about me.

Who was I?

Who was I to be?

I didn't even know where I was born. All the other mice in the Mews seemed to be born within these walls. But something inside me almost remembered another place.

And why hadn't I a name? Surely *Runt* won't do as a proper name. How would *you* like it?

My question mark tail clearly meant that I was of a curious and questing nature. Curiosity killed the cat, which is no bad thing. But for a mouse, curiosity might open many doors. And some of those doors might just have cheese on the other side.

You never know.

YOU WON'T STARVE in the Mews. If you're nowhere near your nest by teatime, there's always what falls out of the horses' nosebags: oats and bran and bits of carrot. On a good day, a lump of sugar.

I was nobody's child. But all mice have aunts, and I had rather more than I needed. I didn't suppose they were my real aunts. But they nested me where they lived and worked, down below the cobblestones of the Mews courtyard, in the needlemice workroom.

Here is the Great Truth and the Central Secret of the British Empire. I'll just mention it now because if you're human, you won't have heard:

FOR EVERY JOB A HUMAN HOLDS,
THERE IS A MOUSE WITH THE SAME JOB,
AND DOING IT BETTER.

All my needlemice aunts sewed the day away, ate a simple supper from leftovers, and slept on their worktables at night, wrapped in remnants. They pleated. They patched. They took tucks and tailored. They wove nets to catch butterflies, for the wings. Their lace was finer than spiderweb.

With gold and scarlet threads pulled from the upholstery of royal coaches, they sewed mouse-sized military uniforms. They had a small operation going in the making of leather belts and holsters. And once, mysteriously, they fashioned a very small saddle complete with cunning stirrups.

They kept their beady eyes on me, especially the Head Needlemouse, my aunt Marigold: She had eyes in the back of her head, behind her listening ears. She was everywhere I turned.

Her snout was spiky with gray bristles, and there were always pins in her mouth. Her fur had gone patchy. She had never been a beauty. But sharp? So sharp, you'd think she slept in the knife drawer. And like all aunts, she was full of sayings.

One of them was: "Ask no questions and you'll be told no lies."

But I was full of questions.

"Why haven't I a name?" I inquired as soon as ever I had the words.

"Nameless is Blameless," Aunt Marigold answered briefly.

"Where did I come from?" I dared ask, though she was apt to snatch me up by the tail if I began to whine.

"I found you under a cabbage leaf," she said, looking aside. She always looked aside when she wasn't telling the exact truth.

I waited. The pins worked in her mouth. "A stork was involved." Again she looked aside.

I waited some more. Then she said, "I brought you home one day in my mending basket because your mother had died." This time she met my gaze.

Then I had a memory of my own—almost a memory. "I remember someplace very warm. Toasty."

"That would be the stove," said Aunty, starchy as her apron. "I put you in a ring box and slid you under the housekeeper's cooker. Otherwise, you'd never have lived. You were touch-and-go, right from the start."

"I can't remember before the stove." I allowed

my lower lip to quiver. "I can't remember my mother."

"How could you?" Aunt Marigold replied. "Your eyes weren't open. They're barely open now. And your mother wasn't from the Mews. She wasn't one of us." Aunt Marigold's pins bristled. "But never mind about all that now. Least said, soonest mended."

This was her favorite saying. And there was nothing wrong with her mending. She mended for the palace itself, and her buttons never came off.

She could sew a fine seam. You had to give her that.

When she packed me off to school, the Royal Mews Mouse Academy, she stitched up my uniform herself. On her own time, late into the night down in the needlemice sewing room.

The Royal Mews Mouse Academy was absolutely the last place I wanted to go. It would take up my valuable time.

"I don't see no earthly reason for school," I remarked unwisely.

"That's reason enough for going right there," Aunt Marigold responded.

I was beginning to whine, always a mistake. She removed a bit of gold thread from her scissor teeth and snatched me up by the tail, quicker than I could think. I was small for my age, or any age. She hoisted me aloft to look me square in the eye. My tail was no question mark now. It was taut as a fiddle string. You could have played "The Blue Danube" waltz on it.

When she had my undivided attention, she said, "Your head's empty. You're to learn how to read."

But what was there to read here in the Mews except the horses' names over their stable doors? I knew those names already. Jason, Xenophon, Morning Star, Bucephalus. Names like those.

Wisely for once, I hung there in silence.

"And remember," Aunt Marigold said. "No fighting at school. You're too little to win."

Ah, she had me there. Silently I swayed. My tail turned tingly in Aunty's mighty grip. Her ebony eyes bored into me. Then she reached for my uniform, and I dropped down on all fours.

Out of her grasp, I dared to squeak, "Surely you won't pack me off to school without a name." I looked up at her, all ears and eyes, very pathetic.

"They'll think of something to call you," she said.

And so they did. In fact, they thought of several things to call me. But mostly Mouse Minor because even then I was always the smallest. But you could hardly call it a name.

"And remember who you are," said Aunty, stuffing me into my new school uniform with the smart gold thread crest on the pocket.

She must have meant I was her nephew, so I

Aunty's apron crackled as she buttoned me into my blazer
and gave a tug to my coattails.

wasn't to shame her. But boldly I blurted, "Who am I?"

Aunty's lips were tight and pursed, over her scissor teeth. Her apron crackled as she buttoned me into my blazer and gave a tug to my coattails.

# Mouse Minor at School

TWICE—EASILY TWICE—that pocket with the smart gold thread crest got ripped off in fights at school. The first time in a tussle with Trevor, the son of the Mouse Comptroller of Stores. He was overgrown, was Trevor, easily three times my size.

"Who do you think you are, you miserable little git? You noxious nobody." Trevor's sneers drew a crowd. "One day I shall be Mouse Comptroller of Stores. My father cannot live forever. And what will *you* be, I should like to know. A *seamstress?*"

Trevor's face was in mine, and all around us the crowd of scholars exclaimed, "Ha-ha. Well said, Trevor. Jolly good. That's telling him." Etc.

*Noxious nobody* indeed. I was of course not going to put up with that kind of talk. Not even from one who was virtually rat-sized. I looked far up at hulking Trevor, propped my spindly fists on my hips, and squeaked, "Listen, you great nincompoop. Your father, the so-called Mouse Comptroller of Stores, is a well-known crook and a thief in the night. He's selling palace cheese on the side and pocketing the profit."

I don't know where I got my information. But the gathered crowd was interested. Trevor's eyes narrowed and reddened. "As for your mother—"

Those were my last words in this first run-in with Trevor. He fell on me, and the day went dark. When I was conscious again, the crest on my uniform hung from a thread, and one of my eyes was far bigger than the other one.

Then when I went a round of fisticuffs with

Fitzherbert—son of the Mouse Permanent
Superintendent of the Mews—he ripped off my
pocket *and* loosened one of my teeth. One of the
two front ones, naturally, one of my best teeth.
He was easily four times my size, was Fitzherbert, and smelled of drains.

When I pointed this out to him and remarked
that he could be smelled from the far end of the
Mews when the wind was right, he pinned me to
the floor. He was all over me, and the smell was
staggering. Now he was speaking moistly into
my free ear. His knee was in my back.

"You do not know your place, Mouse Minor,
you unpleasant morsel of cat meat. Mere nephews ought not be allowed. *Never* nephews." And
once again the day went dark.

From the first morning of my schooling to
the last afternoon, I mixed it up with the sons
of all the best families in the Mews: all the mice of
merit, all the rodents of rank. One or the other
of my eyes was blacked most of the time. Both

He was easily four times my size, was Fitzherbert,
and smelled of drains.

my ears got notched. I was quick with my fists and a little undersized and nobody's child. And I spoke before I thought. It didn't help that I had a better-looking uniform than theirs.

With a heavy heart and a packed lunch somebody was sure to steal, I slumped each morning through the tunnel to school, dragging my question mark tail. I was stuffed into my uniform. Underground and within the walls and in the dark of night, we're often dressed. It's only where humans might see that we're all fur and four-legged. The less humans know, the better.

Time crept like a snail. The days limped by. Aunt Marigold had to let out my uniform, then make me a bigger one. Then a bigger one still. But I was really quite a runt unto the sudden end of my school days.

I rarely met anybody on those sad underground journeys through the tunnel to school every blasted morning. Apart from the occasional slimy slug, leaving its silvery trail behind it. And once or twice a furry caterpillar. Twice, actually.

THE ROYAL MEWS Mouse Academy kept in an airless burrow under the riding school for the human children of the royals up in the palace. We scholars sat below the thump of pony hoofs, occasionally pulling each other's tail, through the long school days. Posture counted. We had to sit up straight on our haunches, which gave me a crick in the back and a pain in the neck.

Our seats were alphabet blocks that had vanished from royal nurseries far above us. Our desks were foot-long rulers. We learned our letters by looking under each other, and we learned our numbers from the rulers. And of course mice are famous for our multiplication.

Our ancient headmaster was peculiar even for a teacher. Not a fine figure either. He crouched on a platform before us with his silk robe black as night wrapped tight around him. He had a nasty habit of swabbing out his ears with his thumb. His fingers were like the spindly spokes of a miniature umbrella. When he pointed one of these dismal digits at you, you shrank and drooped. I did.

Even his teeth were worrying. And you saw them when he sneered. Not big teeth at the front in the normal way, but a lot of teeth, crowding his mouth. Very worrying.

Worse, he had it in for me from the first day. No question about it.

I felt his old, dim, ruby eyes boring into me through the smoked lenses of his spectacles.

In my opinion, you're either English or you're not. We took him for a foreigner. The nameplate on his desk read:

B. CHIROPTERA

and following that in flourishing letters:

*M.A.*

This stood for Master of Arts. I don't know about that, but he was certainly master of the toothpick, as my knuckles proved. Just let my mind wander for a second, and *wham* went the toothpick in old B. Chiroptera's webby hand down on my knuckles with a painful thwack. Yes, mice have knuckles, and mine were swollen up like raisins half the time. My ears scalloped, my eyes mismatching, my knuckles raisins— would it never end?

I'll say this for him, old Chiroptera. He knew his history, backward and forward. And of course human affairs have always been entirely dependent upon mice.

For old Chiroptera, history was always the worst of times, never the best. Even in his reedy, cheeping voice like a rusty hinge he had us on the edge of our alphabet blocks with his lecture on *Mice of the French Revolution.*

It wasn't just human heads that rolled. Never think it.

Down came the razor blade of many a miniature guillotine: *chop!* Mice necks are not easy to find, but the guillotine found them. Many a mouse head, suddenly separated, dropped into the fatal basket, whiskers still twitching—or went rolling across the slick cobblestones of Paris. Severed heads, sightless eyes seeming to stare! Three blind mice and then some more. In all his lessons, old Chiroptera was on the side of the aristocrats and royalty, but this did not stop the chop of the guillotine in his tales.

Boys like blood, but even Fitzherbert and Trevor were scared witless, though they were twice the headmaster's size.

And while he must have been foreign, he seemed to have swallowed the English dictionary. You never heard so many unnecessary words in your life.

"Unaccustomed as I am," he often cheeped, "to scholars as pusillanimous, unprepossessing, even preposterous as you lot, I can only hope to insinuate some nuggets of knowledge into the minuscule cavities between your heedless ears."

Oh, it was a grim place altogether, was the Royal Mews Mouse Academy. I can't tell you—almost preposterously awful.

Behind old B. Chiroptera at the front of the burrow hung a portrait of Her Majesty Queen Victoria. It had been gnawed out of a picture postcard and hung in a place of prominence. Over it was draped a banner to proclaim her Diamond Jubilee: Sixty Years Upon the Throne.

I hadn't imagined her like her picture. I'd thought she'd be wearing a crown and floating on a cloud. Something like that. I thought she might be eating cheese.

We squeaked the school song in chorus every morning to start the day. Most of our voices had changed, though few for the better.

> *Beneath the hoofs,*
> *Within the walls,*
> *We lurk prepared*
> *When duty calls.*

*We are not moles,*
*We are not voles,*
*And thankfully there are no trolls.*
*We're mice who labor all unseen,*
*We're mice in service to the Queen.*
*God save the Queen, and all her relations,*
*And keep us meek in our proper stations.*

Then three halfhearted hurrahs and a weary cheer, and we fell to our studies and pulling each other's tail. All the while, this old human lady stared down at us from her picture. Her eyes in their saggy sockets seemed to follow me.

I DID NOT care for school. But sore knuckles will cure a wandering mind. I learned my letters and how to string words together. Look at this page. And I learned my numbers up to twelve— as far as the ruler went.

We had to know the whole history of Queen Victoria too, her entire family tree all the way back to the roots, all the way down to the twigs. I learned everything except who I was.

But friends? No. There I sat dreary day in and dreary day out, fidgeting at the end of my ruler at the number twelve mark with nobody wanting to sit next to me at eleven.

The eyes of old Queen Victoria seemed to find me even there. She was the greatest queen in human history, and all-powerful. Also very sharp-eyed for a human. Maybe she was all-knowing too. Maybe she knew who I was.

That notion took root there in the minuscule cavity between my notched ears. And there that notion grew and grew as the Queen's jubilee grew nearer and nearer.

# CHAPTER THREE

# Two Crimes

YEARS SEEMED TO pass, though years can't do that among mice. But you know how time seems to stand still at school. Then my school days were over—in a twinkling. I broke two rules when one would do. And the timing was not good. It all happened only two days before Queen Victoria's great jubilee. If I could just have held out a day or so more, there'd have been a school party. With cake. Cheese cake.

But Trevor and Fitzherbert were finally fed up with me. They seemed to think I was the culprit who stuck a caterpillar—a young one just furring out and not quite alive—in each of their packed lunches. Though they could prove nothing.

Rumor reached me that the minute our teacher's back was turned, they meant to pound me into a jelly to discourage my school attendance. Don't be different unless you want your brains battered out.

And so when Trevor and Fitzherbert filled up the school door that dark morning, I turned tail on those hulking hearties making four fists— and on a formal education.

Blindly I fled. I tore back down one tunnel and up another, feeling hot bully breath on my hindquarters. I scampered like the wind with my tail in the air and my heart in my mouth, until Trevor and Fitzherbert and school fell away behind me. Then I skidded into dazzling daylight.

I blinked and drew up. My feet tangled in tanbark. All around me came the pounding of hoofs and the voices of humans.

I froze, one hand to my throat. Somehow
I'd blundered right out onto the rough ground
of the riding school for royal children. It was a
vast room as big as all outdoors. Flags flew all
round it for the Queen's Diamond Jubilee. I'd
skidded to a stop beside the long oval track.
Ponies pounded around it, manes flying, dust
rising. I couldn't budge, not out here in the
glaring open. Sometimes if you keep your
head down, you'll look like something the
horse dropped. There were droppings quite
near me.

Round and round the ring the perky ponies
cantered. On each one of them a human Prince-
ling or Princess of the Royal Blood. We'd learned
them in school, from old Chiroptera. Droves of
them and little foreign royalties too, here for
the jubilee. Belgians, Danes, all sorts. They'd be
eating cake, and plenty of it. They'd be stuffing
their royal faces.

Harnesses jingled. Leather sighed. I was

Round and round the ring the perky ponies cantered.

entirely too close, but dared not move. We were in the middle of a class. The young royals had to ride with their hands gathered in their laps to learn how to give themselves firm seats. The young princesses rode side-saddle, working hard to keep their balance. They carried small whips they could not use, to occupy their hands. Posture counted. In royal circles posture always counts.

I drank in all these smells of pony sweat and leather polish. The whisking tails, the well-bred whinnies. The royal hands clasped in their royal laps. Real life beats school every time.

It was only myself out there, taking it all in like a small bright-eyed horse dropping. And far from where I should be. Far.

A halt was called, and grooms darted out, carrying wooden hurdles. The riding master bellowed another command. The ponies shook themselves, nickered, and aimed at the hurdles. Now the young royals had to clear their fences.

The hurdles were low, only a ruler off the tanbark. But it wasn't at all easy.

A hurdle stood across the track quite near me.

Around came little Maurice, Prince of Battenberg. He was well-fed but so short that his small booted feet stuck straight out above his pony's round sides. The stirrup irons flapped uselessly.

He set his jaw and made it over, though I expect you could see daylight between the saddle and the Prince.

Then here came his older sister Princess Ena of Battenberg. Though not quite a grown-up young lady, she was decked out a treat in her black habit and a hat like a silk cylinder. Her knee in the leather-bound skirt hooked over the horn of her saddle. As her pony cleared the hurdle, her hands were down and her chin was up. One of her nostrils flared like the pony's. She wasn't a Queen's granddaughter for nothing.

Then her pony shied, shuddered to a halt, and nearly shrugged her off.

And why? Because he sensed me there and didn't know what to think. These ponies are well-trained but brainless. They can take commands, but any little thing confuses them. And I was a little thing.

A hoof jittered and drew back. Princess Ena swayed. All her instincts were to reach for the folded reins, to start the pony with a touch of her boot. But she sat unmoving. Now she was looking down to see what spooked her pony. Down, down she looked. And there was I, looking back. Her eyes grew larger.

I had never met a human gaze, let alone a royal one.

I was hypnotized, or very close. Time stopped. Now Princess Ena's eyes were saucers. A gloved hand stole up to her mouth.

And I saw what she saw. I wasn't all fur and four-legged. I was sitting back on my haunches, practicing good posture like hers. I rose and bowed, of course, from the neck, as you do. I might have said something. I usually did, but the rule is that royalty always speaks first. She screamed.

I was in my Royal Mews Mouse Academy blazer with the gold thread crest. I was dressed, and you dare not be where humans can see. It isn't done. It raises too many questions.

The pony stamped and curved his neck.

From on high the riding master's voice boomed: "Keep his head up!"

The humans in the stands—nannies, governesses, tutors, humans like that—were on their feet.

But it was too late to keep the pony's head up. It was down, and he was bucking. His rear hoofs were in the air, and so was Princess Ena, taking a tumble over the tossing mane and arching head. The pony sucked wind, and Princess Ena plunged toward tanbark. Her whip spun in the air, her skirts flared. Cries rose from the sidelines. She hit the ground and sprawled.

Her silk cylinder hung from a hat pin. And I was gone.

I zigzagged like lightning away, down the nearest mousehole. I fled as if something was pursuing me—hot upon my flailing tail. Down in the darkness I was *surer* something was there behind me.

But I dared not be found. Not only had I run away from school, I'd let a human see me dressed. Two crimes, one of them unforgivable. Life as I'd known it was over for me.

Finished.

I TUNNELED THE day away, up one mouse road and down another. Down, down beneath the Mews. Whenever I met another mouse passing by, I turned my face to the streaming wall. Somewhere I shrugged out of my uniform and hid it away within the earthworm earthworks.

I couldn't go back to school, not back to old B. Chiroptera and the Four Fists. And I couldn't go back to the needlemice workroom and Aunt Marigold. I'd let her down. I could only lurk. And after a while I was hungry.

From the courtyard cobblestones above me came the thump and thunder of horses and carriages as the rehearsal for the Diamond Jubilee went on and on. Everybody had a job but me. Throughout the British Empire mice and humans alike unfurled their banners for the approaching jubilee. Everybody but me. I was about as low as I could get.

And that was before I met the cat.

# CHAPTER FOUR

# Evening Stables

B Y THEN THE shadows of afternoon would have been reaching across the Mews, far above. It must have been nearly time for Evening Stables, when the horses are fed and watered and bedded down for the night. I could have used some feeding myself. I'd left my packed lunch in my uniform.

Somehow I found myself at large along the Old Kent Road, the major Mews mouse thoroughfare, about three rulers under the cobblestones. It's a dual carriageway, the Old Kent Road, and far too public.

Big enough to echo. I ought to have been holed up somewhere tucked away, amongst the black beetles, listening to my stomach rumble.

Then I looked up, and there was the cat.

The great ungainly fluffy thing filled the entire space, moving in a crouch, coming my way. Her matted fur swept the tunnel sides. Her waxy pink ears were bent back along the tunnel top. Her eyes glowed like lamps. Cats see in the dark, though not as well as we do. She had no name, of course. Mews cats don't. It would give them ideas above their station.

And there was I just off the end of her leathery nose. I know what you're thinking. Cats. Mice. She was certain to pounce and have me for her tea.

But no. That may be the way of the world, but it's not how the Mews works. After all, we're in the service of the Queen and all her relations, so we have to rub along together.

I'd need to plaster myself against the tunnel wall and be swept by her filthy fur as she lumbered past. But when she saw me, she stopped. And whinnied. Threw her head back as far as possible, loosened her lower lip as much as possible—and whinnied.

A simple meow would have sufficed, but she worked with the horses, up in the stables. She may even have thought she was one. They put a cat in with a restless horse overnight, to calm it down. And if a cat doesn't do the trick, they put in the goat. Everybody has a job. Everybody but me.

Being a Mews mouse, I have some horse in my blood, but I never thought I was one. I didn't whinny. I never nickered.

I sneezed. I'm allergic to cat fur, and hers was full of chaff from the stables.

There's not a lot to a mouse sneeze, but the cat looked down at me. She blinked her great yellow-moon eyes, sucked a fang, and spoke. With our long history, cats and mice have something of a common language. And her language was common indeed. "Well, look what the cat dragged in, so to speak," said the cat. "Mouse Minor himself!"

I drooped. I'd been making myself scarce all the livelong day, and the cat knew me at a glance. The *cat*. A droplet formed at the end of my nose. The cat's eyes rolled over me. "Truant from school!" she brayed with a slight whinny and a small smirk. "You've blotted your copybook for good and all."

News travels fast in a mews, and cats are terrible gossips. This one was. I supposed she knew all about me and the Prin—

"Pity about Princess Ena," the cat observed. She was breathing all over me and there was treacle on her breath. "The Princess took quite a tumble." The cat sucked her other fang. "They say she must have been knocked senseless. Swears she saw a strange, misshapen little creature wearing—"

"Yes, all right, all right," I said. I was just about at the end of my string. "It was me. I've blotted my copybook and burned my bridges."

"Haven't you just!" said the cat. "Still, it makes a good story. Tell me all about it—straight from the mouse's mouth." She drew her paws together and settled before me. There was no way round her, the great fluffy, untidy thing.

With a sigh, I talked us through my dreadful day: Trevor, Fitzherbert, the canter, the hurdles. Princess Ena in the air.

The cat heard me out, though she was not deeply moved. Cats aren't. "Yes, well, as I understand it," she said, "they're all at sixes and sevens at the Mouse Academy, wondering where you've got to. Rumor has it, the headmaster has set aside a fresh supply of toothpicks with your name on them. There's talk of sending out search parties. I wouldn't like to be you when they find you." The cat grinned.

I whimpered. I couldn't help it. Dared I look back to see if a search party was gaining on me, up the Old Kent Road? It was just the cat talking, but still . . .

"You're all washed up in the Mews," she remarked, "as I need hardly tell you. You'll have to try your luck elsewhere."

Elsewhere? "Elsewhere?"

"Outside the gate." She rolled her eyes in a direction.

But I'd never been outside the gate. It was London out there, a great city wrapped in pea-souper fog swirling round our walls. A sleepless city of clattering carts and smoking chimney pots and the striking of church clocks over crowded graveyards. A city of night even at noon.

I began to whine. "But I don't know anybody out there."

"Quite," said the cat. "Better still, nobody knows you."

I cowered. Never turn to a cat for consolation.

"There's a great world out there," said the cat. "All except the palace." She meant Buckingham Palace that rose like a mysterious mountain above the Mews. But the Mews and the palace were strictly separate worlds. "The palace is no place for the likes of you."

How sure the cat was. But then cats are. "I can't crouch here gossiping," she said. "It's time for Evening Stables. I had better stir my stumps. Some of us have jobs."

But all she did was yawn, the lazy thing. I could see inside her enormous mouth, all that pinkness disappearing down into circles of darkness. She stretched out a paw within a whisker of where I drooped, and worked her furry shoulders.

"They're bringing in another horse from the country, from Windsor Castle," she remarked, "to help draw the Queen's landau for the jubilee procession. And a new horse will need settling in. You know horses—very skittish. And there's something wonderfully calming about me.

"It's a gift." She preened.

Then she whinnied a sigh as if she had a night's hard labor before her. Though all she ever did was settle into the manger and sleep till Morning Stables whilst the horse grazed around her.

"I suppose you'll be wanting your supper," she was saying. "Flatten yourself against the wall and let me pass. Then fall in behind me. It's about the best you can do in the circumstances. Beggars can't be choosers. Any port in a storm. Besides, they won't think to look for you in a manger. It will buy you some time."

We crept along the Old Kent Road, I behind the cat's sagging hindquarters and her swaying tail. In no time at all we'd eased up through a pair of loose cobblestones in the south block stables. Her rear left paw sprang off my head, and up she went, barely squeezing through a space, leaving a circle of loose fur behind—the only grooming she got. I sneezed.

We were in the open courtyard of the Mews, behind a growing pile of manure. It was Evening Stables. The grooms were mucking out and bringing pails of carrots and mash. The stable-hand mice were just as busy, scampering hither and yon, spotting for fallen horseshoe nails and twists of wire and anything that might do a horse a mischief. In all their quick skitter, no human would notice they were at work. For every human on earth, there's a mouse with the same job. This is well understood, unless you're a human.

A ruckus had just broken out. Human voices blared.

A groom went hurtling backward out of a loose box and lit hard. You could hear the air go out of him.

The cat's ears rose to perfect points. We peered around the manure pile. Another almighty crash, there in the third stall along. A horse was bucking, trying to take the place apart. All the hands stood clear. The horse, a new one, was throwing his hindquarters so high that he was about to "come right over" as the saying goes.

They'd already tied a knotted rope to his lashing tail. That's meant to keep a horse from kicking, but nobody had told *him*. We saw only his hindquarters—a Windsor Grey and of course as big as a house. Horses are. It gave the cat pause, so to speak. Her backside swayed thoughtfully. I was tucked up beside her, though her fur was full of things with wings going in and coming out.

The horse kicked out again, trying to get at the grooms. The rest of the Mews went about its business. The cat bided her time. The horse began to quiet, though no human went near that great bulging backside. This was about as close as I cared to be.

But it was time the cat reported for work. "Stay right behind me, under my tail. Move when I move," she muttered.

Under her tail? "I'd rather not if you don't mind," I said in a somewhat mousy voice.

"Do you want your supper or don't you?" Her mouth hardly moved. She was already creeping forward, moving low over the cobblestones. Her ringed tail stood straight out behind. I fell in under it. We crept, eight-legged across the busy courtyard. Human feet in big hobnailed boots tramped around us. Stable-hand mice skittered. Carriage wheels turned.

It was very dank, there under the cat's tail. Worse yet, she stopped short once, and I was nearly faced with disaster. She took her sweet time, getting where she was going. But then we were outside the third stall along. She was winding her untidy self around the boots of one of the stable hands. You know how cats will rub round humans' feet and lean into their ankles. She did that.

I was a busy mouse, trying to keep out of sight under her tail, swerving this way and that. I kept meeting my tail coming back.

A human's voice above us roared out, "There's my old kitty then. Puss, puss, puss." A great gloved hand came down to catch her up, under her saggy midsection. It was a groom about to sling her past the horse into the manger. In the nick of time I grabbed for her tail with both hands. My feet left the paving stones. We were in the groom's grasp. Then we were in the air, flying like a comet with something clinging to its tail. We arched over the enormous horse and lit in the manger.

All cats land on their feet, except this one. She hit face-first and sprawled. I fell off her tail and got the wind knocked out of me.

We were splayed amid the manger hay and the flung carrots. I was stuck all over with bran, and numb with fear. We were *this close* to the flaring nostrils and grinding molars of the Windsor Grey. His head was three rulers long. Maybe four. And those teeth—like great yellow grindstones. He nuzzled his muzzle into the manger hay between the cat and me.

Does he eat mice? That's all I could think of. *Does he eat mice?*

THERE WAS A bit of carrot just off my left cheek. But why eat if I'm to be eaten? My appetite was

Does he eat mice? That's all I could think of. *Does he eat mice?*

gone. The cat resettled in a circle of herself. She did something offhand with her tail.

"Shift over," a deep voice said to her. "There might be a lump of sugar in there somewhere."

It was the horse. The *horse*. Horses have language, of course. Though I supposed it was only whinnies and short answers. But full sentences? Verbs? I couldn't believe it and was struck dumb for once.

"Over you go," he said, licking the cat to one side and rooting deeper with his gigantic black nose. He'd galled a shoulder. It had taken something to get him all the way from Windsor, wherever Windsor was.

"Here, not so rough," said the cat, thrust to one side. "It's my job to calm you down, you great lumbering lummox. You don't want the goat put in, do you? I could make it happen—howl and hiss till they send for the goat. Just say the word."

"I won't have a goat. They smell," the horse

said with his mouth full. Oh, those grinding molars. "I've already kicked a cart to matchsticks today. Broke the shafts and dented the dash rail. I'd make short work of a goat. There'd be nothing left but a pair of horns and a set of hoofs."

I whimpered. But the cat said in her most soothing voice, "What makes you so restless?"

"Nothing much," said the horse. "But I like to make myself known as I'm just coming on duty. After all, I'm to pull the Queen's carriage all the way to St. Paul's Cathedral. I'll need to show my best, as *she* won't be up to much. Poor old soul. She's already got one foot in the grave. She'll do well to live through the trip."

I stared through straw. The cat goggled.

"She's pushing eighty, the old Queen. Human years, but still." The horse chewed thoughtfully. "She's blind as a bat and deafer than a post. And lame? It takes a block and tackle to heave her into her carriage and an act of Parliament to heave her out again. She's on her last legs, is the

Queen. If she was a horse, they'd put her down."

You don't see a cat that shocked every day of the week. Even her whiskers looked scandalized. "I'll thank you to remember you're speaking of the—"

"Well, she's only human, isn't she?" remarked the horse, dribbling feed.

"Indeed she is not," snapped the cat. "She rules by Divine Right. And . . . and a touch of her hand will cure warts." The cat vibrated.

"You still believe that old saw about warts?" said the horse. "I thought that went out with Queen Ann."

The cat stared into space. I doubt if she knew much history. Cats aren't schooled. It would give them ideas above—

"I forget how you lot are here in London," the horse said. "Butter wouldn't melt in your mouths. It's all bowing and scraping in London. But Windsor's proper horse country. The old Queen and I have an understanding. She likes a good horse, and I am one. She very likely sent for me personally."

"As if the Queen had nothing better to do," the cat muttered. But now the horse's eyes went out of focus. He was dropping manure onto his clean bedding. Quite a lot of manure. Steam rose behind him. My eyes watered. The cat had a paw over her nose.

"Ah, that's better," sighed the horse. "Now it smells like home."

Evening Stables were drawing to a close. The blacksmith's hammer had gone silent. Yellow light fell from those high palace windows. Figures of mystery moved in distant rooms. The cat dozed. But then the horse said, "Who's your chum?"

The cat whinnied awake. Her great yellow-moon eyes rolled all over and fell on me. I was trying to bury myself in fodder and oats.

"Who?" she said. "Oh, the mouse? Nobody really. I've brought him for supper."

"Not mine, I hope," said the horse. "I don't eat mice. They're all bones. I've had vole. They're all right. A bit gamey. I've had wombat. Once." One of his great fringed eyes glinted at me. But what could it mean?

The cat arranged herself. She cleared her throat to tell my story. "He has blotted his copybook and burned his bridges. Not content to run off from school, he's shown himself to Princess Ena of Battenberg—in his uniform, if you please. It's expected to kill Marigold, the Head Needlemouse. She calls herself his aunt, though who's to say, really? His origins are murky and his future dark. I've brought him for a bite of supper, out of the goodness of my heart."

"You're too good to be true," the horse remarked to the cat. Then he was looking down and down and down at me. "Have that bit of carrot," he said. "And you might nose round for a lump of sugar. It's yours if you find it." Both his eyes glinted at me now. "There's always a lump of sugar if you know where to look."

"Well, I call that very civil," the cat sniffed, "and better than he deserves. What do you say to the horse?"

I'd never thanked a horse for anything before. Where to begin? I was mealy-mouthed because of the carrot.

"Squeak up," the horse said. "Squeak up for yourself."

"Yes, squeak up," the cat huffed. "Then eat your fill and be off. It's very nearly the middle of the night."

"Nay," the horse said. "I think we'll keep him. Plenty of room."

"A mouse—overnight in a manger?" The cat drew up a paw to her front fur. "There's bound to be a rule against that. Think of the droppings."

"And yet I find him strangely calming," the horse observed.

"Well, I never!" spat the cat. But the horse was already pulling up his left foreleg and leaning into the wall. It was the way he slept, as I was to learn. Before his giant eyes flickered shut, he again glinted both of them at me.

# PART TWO

# The Royal Park

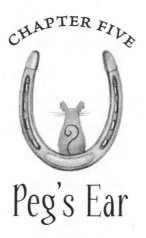

## CHAPTER FIVE

# Peg's Ear

I DREAMED I was late for school and woke to the hot breath of the horse. Though I'd grazed off and on all night long, I didn't know where I was. But my belly was pleasantly round. Gray day was beginning to dawn, and the cat had already vanished. The grooms' housekeeper put down a saucer of milk for her.

"Burrow a little deeper in the straw," the horse said confidentially, "and mind your tail. The stable hands will soon be round to muck out. I'll give the first one a good swift kick, just to let him know who's boss. I'll send him sailing. But then I'll let them groom me. I like that. Mind you stay under the straw. I'll see to it they don't mess about with the manger."

I lurked low as the humans went about their Morning Stables business. After they picked up the stable hand who'd been kicked out into the courtyard, they polished brass and cleaned the exercise harness. One of them stood too near to be kicked and trimmed the horse's heels. I supposed that once he'd been groomed, they'd throw a saddle on him to be exercised. Then I could slip quietly off. But where?

Finally the stable hands clumped back to their quarters to change into their riding gear. "Up you come," said the horse.

I surfaced there at the end of his nose, my ears scooping straw. "No sugar lump?" he asked in his loose-lipped way. "Not to worry. The world's full of them if you keep your eyes open and your nose to the wind. We'll be going out for a turn in the park today, just a quick canter. Only a bit of a trot and a stretch before tomorrow and the main event."

We?

"Time you saw a bit of the world, if you're to find your place in it," the horse said. "Nobody ever learned who he was by staying in the stable."

Who knew a horse had such deep thoughts? And he whinnied less than the cat. They'd given him fresh water, and he sprayed me as he spoke. "Scamper up my face and turn north at the eye. Ride in that ear. You'll just about fit, like the cork in a bottle."

I gaped. I was hip-deep in a manger and stuck all over with oats and bits of straw. And a horse was inviting me to ride in his ear.

"Step lively and show a pair of heels," he said. "The grooms will be here any minute. And mind you hang on for dear life. I'm apt to flick my ears. It's a thing we do, certainly in fly time and if there's a young filly about. No, not that ear. The other one. I'm a bit deaf in that ear, so if you stop it up, it won't much matter. And we won't speak again after I take the bit. Some of the grooms are brighter than they look. Just wedge yourself in and keep your wits about you."

His name was Pegasus. Peg for short. They'd nailed the name on a board above his stall. He'd let them throw a bridle and a saddle on him. Now he glittered in bright brass work. He was blinkered. A worried groom sat carefully astride him. And I in his ear.

It was waxy in there. I slipped and slid before I found my feet. It took all my bravery. I was a mile off the ground. Now we turned to the gate, along with the other horses and riders. Peg led, and his groom had nothing to say in the matter.

Out we trotted under the clock tower in a

river of gray and bay horseflesh into the Buckingham Palace Road. Fog was just burning off a London morning.

I cowered in Peg's slick ear. The Buckingham Palace Road was tangled with hackney coaches and broughams and a thundering great brewer's wagon. Omnibuses top-heavy with humans swayed past. Harnesses jingled. The whole of London smelled oddly like Fitzherbert.

Death beckoned from every gutter and loitered at every turn, under the boots and the hoofs. Humans darted across the traffic. The road sweepers were slapping mud and manure from one side of the road to the other with stumpy brooms. One flick of Peg's ear, and I'd be down in the mire myself, being swept up.

We turned past the grand front of Buckingham Palace. The Queen's own soldiers were just falling in for the Changing of the Guard: bright red and bristling with bayonets. Beavers on their heads. Their boots polished to mirrors. My eyes were out on stalks to take it all in.

I began to look a bit ahead. If I could just hang on here in Peg's ear a day and a night, if I could stop his ear and eat his feed till he was hitched up to the Queen's landau, I might just find my way to the Queen herself. Somehow.

In her infinite wisdom, perhaps she could give me a clue or two about who I was and who I was to be. Worth a try, I thought. I was young. I believed anything could happen.

Round the far side of the palace we started up the broad avenue of Constitution Hill. Ahead was the green blur of Hyde Park we'd learned in geography class.

But I wasn't fated to see it for myself that brightening morning. Oh no.

Now we were high-stepping along the wall of Buckingham Palace's back garden, through a leafy tunnel of trees. I'd never seen an entire tree before—only the odd leaf scudding into the Mews courtyard. The trees sighed in the morning breeze and were very fine except for the squirrels. Great ugly things stuck like leeches to the tree bark, some of them upside-down. Their tails were bushy and flicky and their heads bullet-shaped. Tree rats, really. Mean eyes.

I shrank in Peg's ear, but kept an eye out. Tweedy ladies and tailored gentlemen rode sleek horses up and down Constitution Hill. All very well turned out, humans and horses alike, though none of them a patch on Peg.

Coming our way from the park was a lady riding aside on a fine young chestnut filly. The breeze played in the lady's veils. The morning caught all the lights in the filly's coat. Very dainty for a horse.

She nodded to left and to right. There was a high polish on her hoofs.

A quiver of pure electricity shot through Peg. A moment too late I lunged for the stubble edge

A quiver of pure electricity shot through Peg. A moment too late I lunged for the stubble edge of his ear.

of his ear. The beauteous filly was just passing us when his ear gave an almighty flick, and I rocketed through thin air, completely uncorked and scudding like a leaf.

My hands grabbed at the sky-blue morning. The wind screamed in my notched ears. My tail asked questions all over the air.

Broken glass lined the top of the palace garden wall. I was almost ripped to shreds when by the chance of a lifetime I lit on a low-hanging tree branch instead. Scrambling, I found my balance—blind with fear and all these leaves.

Below me the horses of the Royal Mews clip-clopped on to the park, Peg naturally in the lead. Wait, cried out a tiny voice in my heart.

*Wait.*


I COULDN'T SEE an inch ahead, for the leaves. I could be making straight for a squirrel. You don't know how it feels, being flicked out of a horse's ear into a fully leafed-out tree. You have no idea.

And how suddenly still it was up here, above everything. Almost silent except for a faint, echoing cheep. And a slight susurration. Which is a word off of old Chiroptera's vocabulary list at school. You could look it up. Two *r*'s.

It was better to keep moving. I skittered ahead from one tree tangled with the next. Nothing much seemed to be happening up here, bar the odd ladybug hunting aphids. But somehow I felt eyes upon me. Though not for long, for I found myself on a limb too thin. It bent under my weight. I was full of oats, remember.

The limb twanged, and once more I was in the air with the wind singing in my ears. I lit in a bed of waxy begonias. I don't suppose begonias have ever broken *your* fall, but these broke mine. They were in an herbaceous border within the wall. The sound of the Constitution Hill traffic was faint and far off.

I parted the begonias. I was as waxy as they were, but they were taller. Most things are. I peered out across the private parkland stretching behind Buckingham Palace. The long palace doors stood open to a vacant terrace. Nothing stirred in all this vast garden with its acres of lawn and grove and lake. I hadn't known England itself was this big.

Though it was in the heart of London, there was nothing of London about it. No smell of drains here and only a little wisp of yellow fog drifting in. But this much open country stirs misgivings in a mouse. Birds wheeled high overhead and slid down the wind. With birds you never know. You hear things about birds. Linnets will sing you a merry song. Other sorts snatch you up and drop you on a rock to crack your skull. And magpies will rob you blind. You just never know. There in the distance a bunch of blackbirds were worming the lawn. Four and twenty of them perhaps, however many that might be.

Down on all fours I moved among the begonias, nosing my way forward because there was nothing to go back to. I was in a little shady glade under a tree when I took one step too many.

All at once I was in the air again, dangling just clear of the ground. I hung helpless, swaying in a net attached to a tree branch by a single silken thread. I knew this net. It was one my aunts had made for catching butterflies. Very strong, these nets. You don't get out of them in a hurry—or ever if you're a butterfly.

Unknown hands had rigged this butterfly net with a trip wire. I was trussed tight with my tail trapped. And in the next moment I was staring straight at another mouse. We were nearly nose to nose, though I was upside-down.

I was trussed tight with my tail trapped.

It could have been worse. He might have been a squirrel who took me for an acorn. But no, he was clearly a mouse. And in full uniform, if you please: a scarlet and gold doublet with some sort of motto stitched across his front, a ruff in a starchy circle around his neck, red breeches with a stripe and an opening behind for his tail. Between his ears a black velvet hat with red, white, and blue ribbon remnants. I knew this work too. Very professional needle-work. First rate.

He was fully kitted out as a Sergeant Major of the Yeomice of the Guard. You never saw anything like it—all this scarlet serge and gold braid on a mouse. He had everything but the buckle shoes. I'd often wondered who it was who wore these uni—

"Halt!" he barked, though of course I had.

Before I could squeak up or even think, he was whipping forth a businesslike sword from his scabbard. It may have been one half of a human lady's manicure scissors. Daylight flashed on its wicked edge as he drew back for an almighty swing.

I thought of the French Revolution, and closed my eyes.

# A Life of Drum and Trumpet

NAKED STEEL SLASHING above my ears severed the thread that hung me from the tree. Down I dropped, in a heap. The Yeomouse of the Guard snipped the last threads that bound me. My tail fell in its customary question mark behind. I struggled upright and considered making a run for it.

It wasn't to be. The Yeomouse looked me up and down. Mostly down. "Field mouse?" he inquired. He had a twitch to his whiskers.

I could scarcely believe my ears. "Field mouse?" I drew up to show him my best bearing and perfect posture. *"Field mouse?"*

He seemed to wave me away. "We'll get all sorts here during the jubilee," he said. "Country people in droves up to town for the royal parade. Country mice. Field mice. All sorts. Harmless, most of them, but no business being here in a royal park. And the palace itself is strictly off limits, except to the official and invited.

"We've even had a chinchilla this morning. Would you believe it? Curious-looking cove. Odd ears. All the way from South America, somehow. Didn't speak a word of English. We had to go for an interpreter. Then he said he was looking for the Argentine embassy. I ask you! We escorted him off the premises. It's been that sort of day, and things can only get worse tomorrow."

He was very full of himself, this Yeomouse. Clearly a sergeant major, from the stripes on his sleeve. And I hadn't particularly cared for that field mouse remark. He stroked his whiskers, so I stroked mine—though mine were soft and silky and not the bristles I wanted them to be.

But now he'd sheathed his worrisome sword, so I wondered if I could make an example of him. I made a pair of fists. My knuckles were still swollen from the latest thwacks from the toothpick, so they made a good showing.

"Care to go a round of fisticuffs to see who's the better mouse?" I inquired. This was cheeky, and I'd never won a fight. Still, there's always a first time. He wasn't all that much bigger. He was mostly just uniform. I danced about a bit as boxers do. But then I got tangled in the net strings and fell over.

"Have you any idea how ridiculous you're being?" The Yeomouse's hands were on his red serge hips. "I have the authority to throw you in irons and put you away until the next reign."

"On what charge?" I demanded, staggering to my feet.

"Trespass, for a start," the sergeant major snapped.

This was too much. *"Trespass?"* I pointed my longest finger past him. There on the far horizon was the north wall of the Mews. I was *this close* to home. This far. "I happen to be a mouse of the Royal Mews." I slapped my scrawny chest. "Trespass, indeed. We meet upon my native ground. Practically."

The sergeant major considered me.

"From the Mews are you? Might have known. But if I was you I wouldn't say so, not out here in the world. After all, the Mews is only a barn, isn't it? And smells like one. Come to that, so do you."

The sergeant major smirked. Behind me begonias stirred. A wheeze of muffled laughter rose from back there. I chanced a glance behind to see here and there the black velvet hats and pointed ears of more Yeomice of the Guard poking up from the herbaceous border. Guardians of the wall, no doubt. I was surrounded.

But my spirit was unbowed. "In case you haven't heard, we of the Mews keep the royals rolling. Human and mice alike, we are even now preparing the Queen's landau for her parade tomorrow." I had fluffed out all my fur.

"You astonish me," said the sergeant major, though he didn't look particularly astonished.

"As for smelling like a horse," I continued, "I *arrived* on a horse." I squared up my shoulders, such as they were.

"You came by horse?" The Yeomouse's eyebrows rose. His whiskers nearly twitched off his snout. "Did you ride astride or side-saddle? I'm only asking."

At that, the begonias burst into helpless laughter.

"I rode in a horse's ear and got flicked out," I said with dignity. "Then I dropped off a twangy branch and fetched up in a shady glade."

The begonias were in hysterics now and no doubt falling about. The sergeant major was tearing up. He wiped his eyes. "All right, all right," he said. "Don't tell us how you got here if you don't want to."

"It is the simple truth," I said importantly. "Besides, I am very possibly being followed by a search party. I have the distinct sense of being sought after."

The sergeant major peered around me, in search of a search party. But there was nothing back there but my tail and the giggling begonias.

"And now I had better be on my way. I need to find my horse," I explained. "Who knows how long it may take to catch up with him? On Jubilee Day he'll be drawing the landau with Queen Victoria in it, and I need a word with her regarding a personal matter. I'll thank you to escort me off the premises. Like the chinchilla."

The begonias whooped.

The sergeant major could hardly speak for

laughing, which I found rude. His finger was in my face now. "No, son, you're not going anywhere. We're short-handed these jubilee days. Stretched thin. I can hardly spare the mousepower to put you under guard. Do you know your left foot from your right?"

"Naturally," I said. Surely he wouldn't need proof?

"And can you march?"

"Anyone can," I remarked.

"I don't know about that," the sergeant major said. "You fall over."

"It was the net," I said.

"Are you not yet full-grown, or just short?"

"A bit of both, I suppose." I had already drawn myself up as far as I would go.

"I shall very likely live to regret this, as you seem to have dropped out of nowhere," the sergeant major said gravely. He was the picture of skepticism. Also pomposity. "But how would you like to be a Yeomouse of the Guard? It's either that or you're my prisoner. What's it to be?"

I stared at this so-called choice. A silence lingered. There was only the quietest susurration. And it was from somewhere on high.

I'd hoped to find my fate, but had my fate found me? Was I meant for a life of drum and trumpet and the defense of the palace? A Yeomouse of the Guard? I liked the uniform. It was far smarter than the school blue. And I liked the sword. Useful things, swords, in a world of nets and everybody's bigger.

And so with a small shrug, I lifted my arm and gave the sergeant major a salute with my spindly fingers splayed flat against my forehead.

YEOMEN OF THE Guards—humans—are all very well in their place, as Gentlemen of the Bedchamber and Back Stairs. They have good figures for bowing and scraping. But it takes

Yeomice to guard your boundaries and patrol your perimeters. We're never really off duty, you see. At this very moment that you and I are sharing, Yeomice are on picket and post down among the waxy begonias, guarding the walls of the Buckingham Palace Royal Park. You won't see us, but we'll see you—everywhere you fail to turn.

But it was my fate to be a Yeomouse of the Guard for only a single day. Still, a mouse day is much bigger than yours. We keep busier. We get more done. And a red-letter day, because I made my first friend. Or so he seemed to be.

We had to dress in pairs, to tie the other's ruff at the back of the neck, to arrange his tail around his breeches.

It was Yeomouse Ian who appeared suddenly beside me. He seemed to have thrown himself together in some haste. And there was the slightest whiff of undigested insect hovering over him: But as he was completely kitted out, he was ready to help the new boy. The moment we met, I wanted to be just like him.

He was very grand indeed, was Ian. Not handsome—far from it really. His profile wasn't stirring, but he had that weak and peaky look about the face and under the chin that is the badge of the English upper classes. His whiskers were even wispier than mine, but they drooped with a casual abandon. Very prominent teeth, the pair up front. Very prominent. How nice to be him, I thought—from the first moment we met in the changing room.

He seemed to be kindness itself, in his lordly way, which made a change from Trevor and Fitzherbert and that lot. "You're not to take the sergeant major nearly as seriously as he takes himself," Ian advised. "He's mostly bluster, and he tends to strut. In truth, he's really quite far down the chain of command. I rather suspect him of timidity. The bigger the mouth, the greater the fear."

"Is that a saying?" I asked Ian, admiring it.

"It is now, I suppose," he replied with easy pride.

How gentlemousely was Ian. When he'd helped me into my uniform, he stood back so I could bask in myself.

Mice and men alike look better in uniform than out of it. I looked remarkably good in mine. I stared down my scarlet self, emblazoned with the gold-thread symbols of England, Scotland, and Ireland: the rose, the thistle, and the shamrock, all beautifully worked across me.

And above all, where my chest should be, the Yeomice Motto, picked out in businesslike black thread, though I'm not sure I understood it entirely.

It read:

## SEE, DON'T SAY

Yeomice don't have mirrors. But we have each other. How I longed to be turned out like Ian, down to the last tuck in his tunic.

Mice and men alike look better in uniform than out of it.
I looked remarkably good in mine.

"Shall you be one of the sergeants major one day?" I asked. "Or even the Captain of the Yeomice of the Guard himself?"

"It's very hard to say. I'm rather adrift in the world, being a younger son. It's my older brother who will inherit the title and everything else. And so something has to be done with me until I can find myself in the world. Awkward, really, being a younger son. But one must simply take courage and soldier on."

The thought that Ian too was looking for his place in the world gave me heart, though I was nothing like as grand as he. I was smaller too, though we'd get round to my size soon enough in this conversation.

Meanwhile, I was admiring myself. I liked to think Aunt Marigold had sewn this particular uniform. And the hat too, like a black velvet mushroom, setting off my ears. The very thought of Aunt Marigold, and my eyes went wobbly and moist.

Ian noticed. "It's quite a good fit, that uniform. Might have been made for you. You slipped right in. In fact, you're really rather slick."

"Waxy," I explained, "from the begonias and the horse's ear. I arrived by horse."

Ian cleared his throat behind a polite hand. "It is quite all right if you'd rather not say how you got here."

"It's the simple truth," I said, for all the good that seemed to do.

To change the subject he said, "I'm Ian Henslowe. Rather an old family, actually." Once more Ian coughed courteously behind a hand.

"We came over with the Conqueror. 1066 and all that. And an unpleasant channel crossing by all accounts."

I blinked at all this sudden family history, rolled out like a tapestry. "I can't trace myself back farther than me," I said. "Everything before the warming oven's a blank. My eyes wouldn't have been open yet. Still, I must have had a mother."

"Oh yes, you certainly had a mother," Ian agreed. "Unquestionably."

"And a father," I said.

"Quite." Ian looked down.

"I haven't even a name," I said, taking pity on myself.

"Never mind. Not everyone's named," Ian pointed out. "Take field mice. They never are."

I sighed.

"Besides," Ian said, "Nameless is Blameless."

"So I've heard," I said. "At school I was Mouse Minor."

"Not really a name, when you think about it," said Ian. "And where did you say you were at school?" Now he was helping me slip the cross belt over my left shoulder. And if that was my left shoulder, the foot on that side was bound to be my left foot. It stood to reason.

"I was until recently a scholar of the Royal Mews Mouse Academy."

Ian had drawn me a long-handled halberd from a pool in the armory.

A sword of my own!

Hearing my school, he lurched lightly, but recovered. "I believe some of these minor schools are quite good in their way."

"Quite good," I said. "I know my numbers right up through twelve and rather more about the French Revolution than you'd care to hear."

"Well, there you are," Ian said smoothly. "What more need one know?"

He was a gentlemouse all the way through, was Ian. Courtly, though I had nothing much to compare him to. I wondered if he'd ever been in the presence of Her Human Majesty Queen Victoria, but didn't like to ask. He would certainly know how to act if he were. Besides, I needed to squeak up for my school. "There is nothing *minor* about the Royal Mews Mouse Academy. It is always in the top five mouse schools throughout the British Empire."

"Of course." Ian perked up my ruff and gave my tunic a tug. "All schools are in the top five."

We were stepping up our pace because we'd shortly be on parade. That's military service for you: You're either primping or marching. Ian stood back again to see that I was turned out and standing tall. In fact, I was standing my tallest. I was practically on tip-claws.

"Are you not quite grown or just short?" Ian wondered.

I sighed.

"I do beg your pardon," he said. "That was a personal question, and quite uncalled for. I withdraw it. I suppose you just think of Napoleon and get on with it."

Everyone around us was perking up one

another's ruff and assisting with the arrangement of tails. "Do take care not to tangle that sword in your feet," Ian said. "It wouldn't do to fall over on your first day."

I sighed again.

And before I knew it, we were on our way to the parade ground. And yet more hidden worlds were about to unfold before me.

Many are the mysteries of mousedom.

# CHAPTER SEVEN

# Yeomice on Parade

I'D RATHER HOPED our Yeomice barracks, our armory and mess, would be sunk beneath Buckingham Palace itself. Someplace convenient to Queen Victoria herself. But no. We were quartered at the farthest end of the royal park.

Right at the end of the known world, as far as I knew, among all that bramble and briar.

A woodsy copse, in fact, with so little of London about it that the starlings darted in the treetops, safe from the slingshots of human boys, or the traps of the hungry. Indeed the foliage above teemed with life. It susurrated madly.

Lost in a tangle of rhododendron stands the ruin of an ancient potting shed, far older than the palace. There in its forgotten foundations Ian and I had prepared for parade. Now as we made our way to the grounds, Yeomice swarmed from everywhere. It was rather like that moment with the begonias.

Ian was inclined to stroll when everybody else was hurrying. I noticed that about him. Only a small screen of tree and bush stood between the potting shed and the parade ground beside the lake.

And there just off the path was a mouse grave-yard. You've been past many a mouse graveyard without noticing it, and I'd have missed this one myself, without Ian. We don't have tombstones, you see. They would raise too many ques-tions—questions that could end up in zoology textbooks. But beside a grave outlined by the smallest pebbles Ian drew us up. Then standing his tallest, he presented a smart salute, so I did too.

It was the Tomb of the Unknown Mouse, as Ian explained. There was to be a wreath-laying as part of our jubilee observances. The Unknown Mouse had fallen in some earlier rodent conflict. Cats had been behind it, of course, as cats always are. The world is a hard and warlike place out here beyond the walls of the Mews. I felt a touch of homesickness for my old home.

The other Yeomice scampered by us, adjusting their swords as they went. But Ian led us a little deeper into the mouse graveyard. Under a canopy of spiky holly leaves, scented with pine, were other graves, very faintly outlined. You had to look twice. They were naturally not the graves of ordinary mice, not here in a royal park.

Very little daylight fell upon this hallowed ground. But it was more sad than eerie. Ian lingered beside a grave, and so did I. We didn't salute, but I noticed that he was watching me.

The moment passed, and now we were back on the path, jostling with the other Yeomice on the way to the parade ground. It was nibbled smooth as green velvet all the way to the lake. Handy latrines were dug beneath the holly bush borders. You can't match mice for military efficiency, and covering our tracks.

We were formed up now, chins clenched, rank and file. We don't really have chins, but we clenched what we had. Before us, the lake with Buckingham Palace in the distance.

My tail longed to twitch, even flail, as we waited for the Captain of the Yeomice of the Guard to review us. Being the new boy, I couldn't see a moment ahead. I often can't anyway.

Just when I expected our captain to appear in a blinding puff of colored smoke, he came round to the front of us at the gallop—on a chipmunk.

A chipmunk. I'd never seen one. A sleek and stripy chipmunk, imported at who knows what expense from North America. And he must have been deucedly difficult to break to the saddle. As for the saddle, I recognized it at once.

We are not cavalry, we Yeomice. But what a figure our captain cut astride his personal chipmunk. Evidently he kept it as a hunter. You could hardly imagine him anywhere else but mounted, with the reins easy in his hands and all his leather polished. He drew up, and the chipmunk's eyes rolled. The captain was about to dismount and frighten me out of any growth I had left. But first let us enjoy the moment.

The captain should have been painted and put in a frame just as he was, there atop his skittish chipmunk. He was dazzling in red, glaring in gold. He whose rank descends directly from Sir Walter Raleigh's personal mouse-de-camp.

He was so noble a figure that I could scarcely look at him full on. Every bit of his bearing was living proof of the grandeur mice can rise to. British mice.

Now he had slipped down from the saddle, managing his sword wonderfully. He did something with his tail to reassure the chipmunk before a lackey led the beast away.

Now the captain turned to review us.

We dressed left. We dressed right. The rigid ruff rasped my neck. Tails too are a problem on parade, and mine had a mind of its own. But I was cheek-by-jowl with Ian, moving when he did, stamping and hup-twoing. I liked to think you couldn't tell me from the others. I was just a hair shorter and a beat behind.

But that was over all too soon. The captain had halted before us. Now he called out a blood-chilling question. Just over our head he said, "Any new Yeomice among us?"

*Doomed*, I thought. And about to be found out, so my neck would be for the chop, regardless of ruff.

"Sir! Yes, sir!" shouted our sergeant major, he who'd snipped me out of the trap. "A small one, sir! I don't know if he's not yet full-grown or just—"

"One step forward, the new mouse!" the captain commanded. You wouldn't credit that much lung power to any rodent.

I was hoping to die now. I was that frightened. But beside me, Ian said soundlessly, "Go forth."

I did. One pace. On tip-claws.

Now I was a pace nearer the captain. He had the shoulders of some bigger species. And beneath the gold fringe of his uniform he was all muscle, like a hummingbird.

Even the tree foliage above sighed their admiration.

"Has anyone thought to administer the Yeomouse Oath of Royal Secrecy to this youngster?" the captain demanded.

"Sir! No, sir!" our sergeant major called back bleakly. "We've been stretched thin and short—"

"It is time that runs short," the captain

snapped. "He is either a Yeomouse or our prisoner. What is he to be?"

I felt my sword trying to tangle my feet. Blood drained from my brain and coursed down my wretched body. Only my question mark tail kept me upright.

"A Yeomouse, he!" cried out every squad. Not quite a roar, but very loud.

"Then let him hear the oath," the captain commanded, "and take it to heart!"

Full-voiced, every Yeomouse recited our oath:

> *What we see we never say;*
> *What we learn we hide away;*
> *Whom we serve—a secret deep,*
> *A pledge to her we mean to keep!*

I tried to memorize this oath. There might be an examination coming, like school. By now it was clear that the Yeomousery was a strictly secret force: *See, Don't Say.* That sort of thing, which I'd grasped. But I couldn't see there was any great secret about Whom we served. It was surely Queen Victoria, who was quite well-known. She was on all the postage stamps and pennies. She was really everywhere you turned.

Still, I would have agreed to anything. And I might still drop over dead from sheer fear, so why worry?

"Back you go," said the captain, privately to me. And this tone of his voice stirred me too.

I took a careful step back, despite the sword trying to tussle with my feet. And the tail with a mind of its own. And no blood anywhere near my head. Somehow I was back next to Ian, who said, without moving a muscle: "Jolly good show."

IT WAS TIME to troop the colors. As it happened, they weren't flags. They were twopenny postage stamps bearing the Queen's profile, pasted back to back and flown from matchsticks.

Behind them trooped the regimental band.

Drums small enough for mouse hands are more thump than thunder. And the trumpets sounded reedy, being actual reeds. Still, they thumped and wheezed a proud accompaniment when we all burst into song. "Land of Hope and Glory," of course, the British Mouse National Anthem. Humans didn't get wind of it until years later:

> *Land of hope and glory,*
> *Mother of the free,*
> *How shall we extol thee,*
> *Who were born of thee?*

Very stirring stuff. A lump nearly formed in my throat as our voices rose to echoing cheeps in the branches above. Then something quite unexpected happened.

Through a light lake mist nosed the prow of a boat. Suddenly there it was, just behind our captain. He pivoted on a spurred heel. His hand rose in salute.

It was a toy boat, but a big one—one of those German clockwork tin yachts. Lettered on its bow was *The Prince of Battenberg.* It had no doubt belonged to one of the little Battenbergs—Prince Maurice, perhaps. Quite a number of unknown mouse hands must have removed the yacht from the toy chest in a royal nursery. Princes have far more toys than they need.

We were just coming to the end of a verse of "Land of Hope and Glory":

> *Wider still and wider*
> *Shall thy bounds be set,*
> *God, who made thee mighty,*
> *Make thee mightier yet!*

And then the yacht bumped aground. At the wheel the pilot was an old mouse salt, in full nautical gear. It made sense that we mice have our own navy. Humans do.

A pair of mouse roustabouts in striped jerseys

swarmed ashore, tied up, and lowered a fine-toothed tortoiseshell comb for a gangplank.

We presented arms. My sword was cold against my nose. My nearly crossed eyes beheld a strange sight.

A greatly overweight mouse came tottering down the comb. His legs were no match for his body. He swayed dangerously. The roustabouts handed him ashore. Otherwise he could have ended up in the drink. He'd begun to buckle.

You rarely see a mouse that size unless he's fallen into a butter churn. He was tightly packed into a swallowtail coat over striped trousers. His curly-brimmed hat was a Harris tweed with a cockade of grouse feather. Yellow gloves in one hand, a cane in the other. It was enough to make a begonia giggle.

He might have been quite young. He'd tried to raise a beard, but it hadn't worked. Now he was ashore and waddling his way to our captain.

His legs were no match for his body. He swayed dangerously.

We waited, knees locked, for him to return our captain's salute. Finally he got around to it. But he was wheezing and damp through from walking all that way from the yacht—two rulers away. I had the feeling his clothes were more English than he was.

"Prince Bruno Havarti," Ian Henslowe breathed into my notchier ear.

Prince? How could that be? Havarti made him Danish. And Danish royalty was here in force for the Queen's jubilee. They would have brought along any number of courtiers, some of them mice: Danish Mice Equerries, Rodents of the Bedchamber, Squeakers of the Chamber Pot—whatever. But rodent royalty, even among the Danes?

I couldn't grasp it.

"*And* he's a younger son," Ian imparted, "so he'll be looking for a foreign throne to sit upon."

The whole thing was preposterous. Besides, if he was royalty, why was he alone? Royal can't manage on their own. This one had barely made it down the gangplank. And if he didn't know to travel with his Mouse Equerry, why didn't we provide him with one?

Echoing my thoughts, Ian murmured, "His English equerry was called away suddenly."

Which was a shame, because Prince Bruno Havarti looked miserable. A tea tent had risen suddenly, as it was now teatime. From the flaps drifted the scent of hot scone crumbs and fresh strawberries. Prince Bruno looked famished.

But even he had a duty to perform first. Out of nowhere lackeys appeared, bearing floral tributes. Our captain took up an enormous wreath of dogtooth violets and handed it ceremoniously to the great Dane.

This left the captain with a smaller bouquet of pale violets in his hand.

We Yeomice had formed an honor guard by now. The captain and the Prince walked between us, back to the mouse graveyard, where

Prince Bruno laid the wreath on the grave of the Unknown Mouse.

It was quite moving, though the Prince did not bend well. Then we saw our captain was laying his handful of flowers on another grave. It was the grave where Ian and I had lingered.

It was mournful and mysterious, but just for that moment. Now we Yeomice formed up again to flank the tent entrance. How well we do that sort of thing. Knees locked, ears pointed, ruffs perked. We are all spit and polish, all see and no say. We smelled the fresh strawberries and scone crumbs and our whiskers vibrated. But we were as statues.

How proud I was to be a Yeomouse of the Guard. Little did I know my career was to last no longer than this day now ending. Even now a setting sun struck fire at the windows of the distant Buckingham Palace.

# CHAPTER EIGHT

# Snatched and Dispatched

E VENING DREW ON, and the tea tent was struck. As darkness climbed the trees, their cheeping grew louder, and a silky sighing came from on high.

The roustabouts had long since wound up the clockwork yacht. Now it had sailed away through the mysterious mist, low in the water, as Prince Bruno Havarti was filled to the brim with scone crumbs and fresh strawberries.

I was myself more than ready for dinner.

The Yeomice mess hall was deep down among the roots of a tree that had undermined the ruined potting shed. And so it was rather low-ceilinged and noisy. I was hungry as a Havarti, but the meal hadn't been up to much, though long. A shred of underdone venison, then foot of rabbit. The pudding was a beetle flambé with a flaming sauce that looked like butterscotch, but wasn't.

Still, it was very well served by mice orderlies in paper hats, back and forth to the kitchens. I'd never been served before and quite liked it.

Following the cheese and biscuit crumbs, we were all upstanding to toast Queen Victoria on this, the eve of her Diamond Jubilee.

"To Her Human Majesty," we squeaked, whole-hearted and full-throated.

As the orderlies cleared our crumbs, I wondered when I'd eaten last.

Back in the Mews, it must have been, in the manger, scarfing up the oats and carrot bits from Peg's breakfast. How long ago. How far away. It made me think.

"I ought really to be getting back to the Mews and my horse," I remarked to Ian. "It will be parade time in the morning before we know it." They were serving the coffee now, in scooped-out acorns. "I'm quite determined to have a word with Queen Victoria about who I might be. I'll be very grateful for any insights Her Majesty cares to share."

I don't know how much I myself believed in this scheme. It was a ramshackle plan with more holes in it than a Swiss cheese. But you know how you are at that age. And it helped to say it aloud, to Ian. It made it more real.

"Really?" he said, watching me over his steaming acorn. "Are you under the impression that you can communicate with a human?"

"She isn't human." Didn't Ian know that? "Her powers are magical and unexplained. And . . . a touch of her hand will cure warts."

"My dear chap," Ian said, "I thought that old warts nonsense went out with Queen Ann.

Queen Victoria is quite human, all too human, and nothing whatever to do with you."

I thought this a bit harsh on both the Queen and me. But Ian wasn't finished. "Besides, you are not free to scamper off to the Mews or anywhere else. You have hardly been a Yeomouse long enough to earn leave. In any case, you and I are on sentry duty tonight. We have a stretch of garden wall to walk. Our names are on the roster."

The roster? Really? I didn't see a roster. Still, if Ian said so, it must be true.

He and I were among the Yeomice standing around outside under the foliage, resplendent in our red and gold. A few carried their acorns into the open air. Very convivial, Yeomice. You don't wear your sword to dinner. It isn't done. Dueling could break out between the courses. So now we were strapping on our scabbards. Time drew nigh to relieve the Yeomice finishing their watch on our stretch of the wall.

Not a moonbeam winked in the inky night. But in the distance Buckingham Palace was lit up like a birthday cake. Gas flames flared at every window. Music wafted over the rippling lake.

A grand state dinner at the palace seemed to be ending. The royal guests were spilling out onto the terrace, around the urns. Queen Victoria would have dined more quietly and was no doubt tucked up in her bed by now. Being on her last legs, she could hardly attend a party that spilled out onto the terrace. It took a block and tackle to get her into her carriage, as we know, and an act of Parliament to get her out again.

All these royal thoughts crowded my head, and so my mind wandered, unwisely.

How smooth and manicured the park between the far-off palace and here. Smooth and new-mown and deadly. Being out in the open even on a moonless night is no place for a mouse. Owls, you see. Owls with their awful wingspan and flat yellow cats' eyes, their beaks like guillotines. I'd never seen an owl, but we are born knowing, we mice. Besides, many a mouse has been devoured to his toenails by an owl he never saw. They are that quick. That heartless.

Under the overhang of a holly bush, Ian spoke into my ear. "I must just drop by the latrine before we go on duty. Carry on, and I'll meet you by the wall." How offhand Ian was. "Cut across that bit of open country. It wouldn't do to get tangled up in a net again when you can't see where you step. You fall over, you know. Mind how you go."

Then Ian went. And I started across that open bit of park between the holly bush and the wall. I dropped down on all fours for quick and easy movement, though my sword dragged the grass.

I was no sooner in the open when a thought

gave me pause. Ian had said my name was on the duty roster. But how could that be when I didn't *have* a name? How?

I WAS THIS CLOSE to the wall when I was seized in steely grips beneath both arms and jerked rudely up into the night. I kept running for a moment, paddling in the air. But then my feet and hands hung helpless, and the wind rushed between my toes. I don't know why my heart didn't give out. I don't know how I've lived to tell it.

It was all far worse than being snared in that butterfly net. I squealed. Now I was higher than the wall, higher than the treetops. I squealed like anything for Ian. But had he been the one to lead me into this terrible mousenapping? Was he part of some great plot?

And was I hanging from an owl? Oh, don't let it be an owl. But I'd never before been hung by the armpits from an owl, so how could I know?

We were over the lake now. I saw ripples

silvered by the palace lights and stopped struggling. If I was dropped now, I'd be drowned like a rat.

We wheeled high in endless sky over London, over everything earthly. And we were turning now toward the palace. Snatched and dispatched! Were these my final moments? But somehow I didn't think *owl*. An owl would have had my head off by now. And I didn't think *beak*. Somehow I thought of teeth instead, rows and rows of chattering teeth.

And I seemed suspended from not one creature, but two, flying in close formation. Two heads seemed to flank mine, two heads too close to see. Four ears, nowhere near as big as mine, cocked against the night.

They were winged creatures, or we wouldn't be up here. I sensed the throb of wings beating with a silken sound, susurrating like the treetops.

As we swooped, eyes seemed to glow on either

side: red as rubies, paired and peering, pointing our way through all this rushing sky.

Yes, there were two of them. I felt the beat of their separate hearts beneath the beating of their wings. *My* heart was in my mouth.

They had an odd smell too, and oddly familiar. Mildew and undigested bugs. I gathered they weren't going to eat me in flight. They were saving me for later.

Time was running out, as it does with mice. But quicker. We swooped nearer the palace now, slanting in above the terrace. The cheeping of my captors bounced off the palace walls. My scabbard came loose. My sword fell away. I felt it go, so now I was unarmed, on top of everything else.

The palace party lit the night from below. A babble of human voices rose to join the rush of wings, the steady cheep.

We were making straight for those blank attic windows that frame a deeper darkness than the night. The attics dead ahead. The terrace below, candlelit and ablaze with diamonds. And far too many humans.

A fall from this height would do me in. But we were about to land on an attic windowsill. I peered into the moments ahead: two winged and webbed creatures hunched high in the attic rafters, picking over my bones in perfect privacy.

No! I wouldn't have it!

I must take my fate into my own hands. Now it was time to make my smallness work for me. Somehow I made myself even smaller still. My shriveling arms slipped out of my sleeves. Down I dropped, slick as a whistle, out of my uniform and the grasp of my webby abductors.

We mice live by quick wits and pure instinct, or you wouldn't be reading this.

They flew on, my captors, clutching my Yeo-mouse uniform. I caught only a glimpse of red and gold and wondered one last time if Aunt Marigold had sewn it. But now I was tumbling,

A fall from this height would do me in.

tail over teacup, into the midst of royalty gathered for the jubilee. I dropped like a furry stone, my tail making one last inquiry of the unforgiving sky.

# PART THREE

# The Royal Palace

# CHAPTER NINE

# Midnight

Y OU CANNOT DROP through space and
think clearly at the same time. Cigar
smoke rose in a fog from the gentlemen below.
The tiaras on the ladies' heads were pointed and
diamond-sharp. But I had only a whiff and a
glimpse.

I splashed down and was drenched to the skin.

The lake? But the lake was nowhere near the
terrace. I hit shallow bottom with a painful
thump and rose through bright redness. Blood?
Mine? I swallowed some. Very strong medicine
with a strawberry flavor.

I'd dropped directly into a bowl of punch and even now
was learning to swim.

Surfacing, I cracked my head on a lump of ice. My cap, the black velvet mushroom with ribbons, floated off my head. I'd dropped directly into a bowl of punch and even now was learning to swim.

Directly above, a human towered over the punch bowl and me. A very superior palace servant of some sort. His wig was powdered. In his gloved hand a heavy silver ladle. On his face a look of horror and disgust when our eyes met. I was peering out of the bowl, paddling punch. He hadn't seemed to see me fall in.

With a quick look to either side, this servant ladled me up, along with a fresh strawberry.

I lolled in the ladle, helpless, my whiskers flat against my snout, my tail over the edge. What next?

With considerable presence of mind, the towering servant had me by the tail, pinched between his great gloved thumb and finger. I was trapped in the suede cage of his loose fist.

Then he stuffed me behind himself, down an inside pocket in one of the tails of his coat. Still waxy and now slick with punch, I skidded to the pocket bottom and fetched up in a wadded handkerchief, none too clean.

I was wet through. There's something especially penetrating about strawberry punch. Still, I was out of sight and out of mind, here in the linty pocket bottom.

And here I bounced till all hours as the servant in his flapping tailcoat bobbed and weaved among the guests with his punch cups on a tray. Bowing. Scraping.

With all this tossing about I began to feel peaky and bilious. I had the awful feeling that the beetle flambé might reappear. My whiskers were bent. My tail any old way. My head splitting. I was close to despair and no nearer my goals.

But at long last the orchestra struck up "Auld

Lang Syne," a gentle reminder that the evening was drawing to a close.

The footman or whoever he was stood to attention. And there in his tailcoat, a tiny spark of hope kindled within me.

He was a *palace* servant, was my footman. Buttons gleaming and wig powdered. And we were *this close* to the palace.

A moment later and we were in the palace itself, heading down a spiral of stairs, bearing the sloshing punch bowl to the kitchens. I was under the same roof as Queen Victoria!

My heart didn't sing, but it began to hum a bit.

We seemed to be near the sinks. Crystal clinked. Very damp these underground kitchens. The footman sneezed. It was like a volcano erupting above me. He reached for his handkerchief, and here came his monstrous gloved hand. I shrugged out of the handkerchief and snatched back my tail in the nick of time.

His handkerchief seemed to reach his nose for the second sneeze. I was breathing hard, but he'd forgotten I was there! If he'd remembered, he'd have had me up with the handkerchief. He'd have flung me on the kitchen fire. Hope flared in my pounding heart.

Then gunfire seemed to break out. Serving maids shrieked. But they were corks popping out of champagne bottles left over from dinner. The servants seemed to be helping themselves. I gathered that my footman had a glass in his hand.

"To the Queen, God bless her," he called out. And all the maids replied, "To the Queen!"

My footman must have been standing very near one of the maids. An apron swished starchy over skirts. He was muttering something in her ear.

"Cheeky boy!" She sniffed. Boy? He was tall as a tree even without the powdered wig. "I haven't the time for *that*. I must take up a cup of chamomile tea to Her Nibs."

I was listening hard. I was all notched ears.

"Have a care how you speak of the Queen," said my footman, stiff as his shirt. "Her Nibs, indeed."

"Then what do you suggest?" asked the maid, very saucy.

" 'Yes, Your Majesty,' 'Of course, Your Majesty,' 'Three bags full, Your Majesty,' " replied my footman.

"As if I don't know how to address 'er. And, 'ere, you leave my apron strings alone."

My head swam. Were they talking about Queen Victoria? Was this serving maid about to take a cup of tea to Her Majesty the Queen of England and Empress of India?

I don't know where I got the energy after the day I'd put in. But I was all over that pocket at once, my heart racing on ahead. Now I was scrabbling up and out of the pocket. Chill air rushed at my damp head, my plastered whiskers. I hung, swaying from the inside of the footman's coattail. There were servants all about, washing up and helping themselves to the champagne. I worked my way to the other side of the coattail. Oh how easily the footman could brush me off—into a drain, into that open salt box, into the crackling hearth.

But he stood still and very near the saucy serving maid. "I could, of course, assist you in carrying up the tea to Her Majesty's quarters," said my footman. "Very dark, those corridors, and full of twists and turns."

"You?" said the maid. "You're full of twists and turns yourself. Wot do you think you're playing at?" And then she flounced away. Off she went with a pot of chamomile tea on a tray for the Queen. And it's true, the footman had pulled loose the tails of her apron, the cheeky boy.

And I hung from one of them like the clapper in a bell, clinging for dear life.

HIGH IN THE palace at the end of a dark and twisty corridor is Queen Victoria's bedchamber.

You will never see this room because THE
PUBLIC IS NOT ADMITTED but I can tell
you a bit about it as it was on a certain June night.

The bedchamber was nothing like as fine as
the State Rooms below, or the Picture Gallery.
Cobwebs clung to the corners. The hangings on
the Queen's bed could do with a good shaking
out. Her counterpane had bald patches.

So did she, but Her Majesty was nowhere
near bed yet. She sat at her writing desk in a
rather tatty old dressing gown and four shawls.
Her nightcap clung to the back of her head with
streamers hanging down. A cheery fire glowed
in the grate. Her spectacles were on her nose,
reflecting the flames.

She had opened her diary and taken up a pen
to write words the world would later read:

*How well I remember this day sixty years ago
when I was called from my bed by dear Mama
to receive the news of my accession.*

That meant it was past midnight now. The day of her Diamond Jubilee had come at last. Sighing, she set her pen aside and worked the worn wedding ring on her pudgy hand. A memory of her long-ago husband, Prince Albert, hung in the room like the cobwebs in the corners.

She sighed again and scattered a little sand to dry the page. Then she reached for the cup of chamomile tea the serving maid had brought to her.

Up went the cup in her pillowy hand. And there was I who'd been peering around it, one hand drawn up to my front fur, and my tail questioning the saucer.

She saw me. Her vision was dim even with spectacles. Her milky old eyes looked so loose in their sockets, they seemed ready to drop out and roll around the writing desk.

But she saw me. Her eyes followed the turning of my tail.

"Ah," said the Queen of England, "we rather thought we weren't alone."

Mice have died from less shock. But I drew myself up, as tall as I would go. I showed her my posture. Then I bowed, crisply from the neck, as you do.

# CHAPTER TEN

# Eyes and Spies

YOU NEVER LAID eyes on an older human than Queen Victoria. There may not be any. She bent nearer till she was all I saw. Her many chins drooped. Her dewlaps dangled. I remembered the picture that hung in our schoolroom—how her old eyes followed you everywhere. And I saw it was true, that she was all-seeing, no matter how saggy her sockets.

She leaned so near me I felt the breeze off her breath. We were suddenly back in the cheese course of her supper. I was frozen with fear, my head cramped in its bow.

"What pretty posture," she remarked. "Are you a military mouse? And squeak up. I am quite deaf in both ears."

I quivered. Squeak up? *Squeak up?* Did we share a common language? Could it be that Ian was wrong and I could communicate with a human? Yes!

I quivered into speech. "Yes, I am a military mouse, Your Nibs—Your Royal—Your Majesty. As recently as dinnertime I was a Yeomouse of the Guard."

"Indeed," said the Queen. We were nearly nose to nose now. I saw me twice in her spectacles.

"Then why, might two ask, are you not uniformed in our presence? We trust you do not merely happen to be passing."

My spine throbbed with good posture. I swallowed hard.

"It is difficult to say where my uniform has got to, Your Majesty," I said, squeaking up. "My cap is in the punch bowl. My sword is in the lawn, but my uniform—"

"Is in the palace attics." The Queen pointed a bent, blunt finger to her bedchamber ceiling. "Hanging from a splinter in the rafters."

I gaped. How could she know such a thing? Unless . . . she was all-knowing as well as all-seeing.

"Ah, we hear everything, deaf as we are. And see everything, even in our blindness." The Queen sat back in her chair to examine me from all angles. She worked a thoughtful finger over her chins.

"Talking of uniforms, were you or were you not late a scholar of the Royal Mews Mouse Academy?"

I nearly sagged.

"We have not clung to the throne for sixty years without eyes and spies everywhere. So be careful in your answer. We recommend the truth."

The Queen sat back in her chair to examine me from all angles.

"Yes, Your Majesty," I confessed. "I did attend the Royal Mews Mouse Academy. While I did not care for it, it is one of the top five schools in your empire."

"Yes, yes." Her Majesty waved the teacup. "Aren't they all. But are you not the scholars who wear those cunning blue flannel uniforms with the gold-thread crests?"

"We are, Your Majesty. My aunt Marigold ran up my uniforms personally."

The Queen nodded. "Yes, I believe Marigold does very fine work. The Mouse Duchess of Cheddar Gorge swears by her. You mice are fortunate to have her. Human help is almost impossible to get nowadays. No one wants to work. You see what lazy hounds the footmen are, swilling our champagne in the kitchens."

The Queen drew herself up from the tangle of shawls. Her dewlaps swayed. "But the question before us is this: Are you the same mouse who appeared before our granddaughter Princess

Ena of Battenberg during her riding lesson? And were you not in your school uniform, causing the poor child to take a nasty tumble and seem to talk out of her head? Ena, for whom we have such high hopes?"

I squeaked bleakly and could only nod.

"Have you learned nothing at school, indeed the First Rule? *Never appear clothed before humans. It raises too many questions.*"

"Yes, Your Majesty."

"And the Second Rule of which you seem equally ignorant: *Never appear before any Sovereign Queen out of uniform.*"

I nodded, near despair. I don't think I ever *had* heard that Second Rule, actually.

What a lot of trouble I had gone to in order to stand before my Queen and Sovereign. Then it was the same as being called into the headmaster's office to hear old B. Chiroptera telling you about all your failings and shortcomings.

"You have got off entirely on the wrong foot

in life," the Queen was saying. "You have gone about everything exactly *backward*. Ena should have seen you in fur and four-legged if she need see you at all."

The Queen pointed to her royal bosom. "*We* rule. And so we must know the truth about mousedom—every little thing about *you* little things. But Ena is only an impressionable girl who must be protected from the truth."

I was growing smaller than I was. But the Queen had only begun. "There is a time and a place for everything. In our presence—*should you be summoned*—you are to be turned out in appropriate uniform. Mice, like men, look better in uniform than out of it."

"I fell out of—"

"Then you should have fallen into another one. And why, by the way, are you such an unhealthy color? It is a pink suitable only on a piglet. And why are you spiky with black bits? You look like a misdirected chinchilla."

"We—I am pink from the strawberry punch, Your Majesty," I said, hopeless. "And the black bits are lint from the footman's pocket."

As if she didn't know.

"No, we do not know everything," said the Queen, reading my mind. "But there is nothing we cannot find out. Take that for your motto. It has served us well."

"But that's just why I'm here, Your Majesty." I had one more round of bravery in me, and I fired it. "I've come to Your Majesty to find out who I might be." I tried to make myself look pitiful. "I haven't even a name." Poor me.

The Queen peered over her spectacles. "Ah well, 'Nameless is Blameless.'"

"So they say," I replied, "but I've never quite known what that saying meant."

"Nor have we," said the Queen, "but it rhymes, so that's a comfort. Besides, the name that matters is the name you make for yourself in a life of struggle and success! Consider us. We are only a weak woman and a heartbroken widow, but we have become the most famous Monarch in Europe. Queen of Queens! Empress of Empresses!"

She was half out of her chair and quite magnificent.

"Can you have people's heads off?" I asked, breathless now.

"No, you are thinking of the French," she said. "But I am Victoria by name and Victorious by nature!"

She looked around her empty chamber as if it were thronged by an adoring crowd, cheering. She looked like she might burst into "Land of Hope and Glory," if humans had heard of it yet.

And she wasn't done either. "Our dominion extends over palm and pine, and the sun never sets on it. But once again, you have got everything the wrong way round."

She looked me up and down in that way she had of seeing straight through you. "Of course, you're very young. Are you not quite grown or just short?"

I whimpered.

"Never mind. You have forgotten the Great Truth. And how like you, since you have already forgotten the First and Second Rules." Her eyes bored holes in me. "What *is* the Great Truth?" I heard a tapping that could have been her foot, if it reached the floor. "We are waiting."

I stood there, pinker than a piglet and linty all over. My hands hung down. Then the Great Truth came to me, more or less, and not a moment too soon. Out it spilled:

"For every human on earth, there is a mouse doing the same job, and doing it better."

Her Majesty blinked. "Well, we suppose that's close enough."

Then she waited as I came to a true understanding of the Great Truth. At first I thought, oddly, of the Danish Prince Havarti.

Was that dawn beginning to break at the bed-chamber windows?

At last I knew, *just like that*. The chamber seemed to flood with light. "There is *another* Queen of England and Empress of India," I said, putting two and two together. "And she is a . . . mouse? A . . . royal rodent?"

"Quite," said Queen Victoria, "though it took you long enough."

I grew dizzy. My saucer seemed to spin.

"We are Queen of Queens and Empress of Empresses," said Her Majesty. "But whilst we see everything, we cannot see *to* everything. Only imagine how much this jubilee alone tires us. All these foreign royals like a plague of locusts, eating us out of palace and home. The Belgians alone! Not to speak of the Danes. And the Russians— all that barbaric splendor! *And* I have had nine children, all of them troubling and troublesome. And forty grandchildren. Not a vast number for mice, but an absolute multitude for humans. A veritable *infestation* of grandchildren."

Forty did sound like quite an infestation of grandchildren, however many it was.

"And so you must apply to the Queen of the Mice, not us. Her court is the Great Truth and Central Secret of the British Empire. All very hush-hush because were it generally known, it would raise too many questions. Still, we wonder you did not put two and two together before, as two do."

My head pounded painfully. Should we have been singing "God Save the *Queens*" all this time? And why am I the last to learn anything?

"But is the Queen of the Mice as old as . . . Your Majesty?"

"As old as *we*?" The Queen's spectacles flashed fire. "How could she possibly be as old as we? She's a *mouse*. You are all rather here-today-and-gone-tomorrow, aren't you? That's precisely why *she* must keep her eye on her subjects and not we.

"And since you are one of her subjects, here is a word of advice. Do not cross the Queen of the Mice. She lacks our sunny disposition."

I swallowed hard, one last time. "But where shall I find Her . . . Mouse Majesty?"

"*We,* sadly, are at everybody's beck and call. She is not. Her whereabouts is a part of her mystery. But you might begin one flight up." Again Queen Victoria pointed to her ceiling. "And now you may withdraw. Indeed, you must."

The fire had burned to embers, and the Queen was a bit smaller, though of course still a mountain to me. She was ready for a catnap, if you'll excuse the expression.

Far below her windows, I knew the Royal Mews must be stirring. The stable hands were mucking out. The stable-hand mice were darting this way and that, gathering up horseshoe nails and twists of wire and anything that might do a horse a mischief. Peg was taking the bit whilst the grooms burnished him to a high sheen to lead the Queen's landau, right across London.

It was time to go, but you do not show your back to the Queen. To her, we are all spineless, rodent and human alike. Getting out of the saucer and down from the writing table was going to be a bit of a job. Never turn tail on royalty.

She gathered her hands before her. They were like two small pin cushions, with liver spots. And she watched to see how I'd take my leave. Her gaze was more blue than milky now.

"You did not do wrong in coming to us first," she said. "But do not expect to find all your answers in the first asking." Her mouth pulled into a sharp vee that was something like a smile. A wintery smile, but she was in the winter of her life. "And we suppose we must be grateful that you had not come about warts."

I was just stepping backward out of the saucer, reining in my tail. "But, Your Majesty, *will* a touch of your hand cure warts?" I asked, squeaking right up.

"Do you *have* warts?" she asked, though I was plain to see.

"No, Your Majesty."

"Then we shall never know, shall we?"

# CHAPTER ELEVEN

# A Rush of Black Wings

I'D SWUNG INTO the royal bedchamber on a serving maid's apron strings. But I had to show myself out. The door was nothing. To mice, doors never are. We slip right under the tightest doors in your palace. I especially, being slick and small.

Beyond the dark corridor, the palace was waking. Breakfast crockery clashed, far off, and a kettle sang. The floorboards creaked, warming with the morning, caught between dry rot and rising damp. Mice have very keen hearing, and need it.

My head was heavy from all I'd learned straight from the drooping lips of Queen Victoria. Now I wanted to slip down the nearest mousehole and sleep the day away with my tail tucked. But there was no time for that because you don't get all your answers from the first asking, and so I must ask again. Besides, I had a name to make for myself in a life of struggle and success. Mice don't have all the time in the world.

Heavy human boots thudded behind me. I could only flatten myself against the wall. I might have been a bubble of gray paint along a skirting board. A giant human tramped past. In his hand was a wire cage crowded with flashing eyes and flailing tails.

It was the Royal Rat Catcher, who'd already been round his traps this morning. How useful the Royal Rat Catcher, as rats have no real language apart from whining, and they'll eat anything smaller than they are. And think of the droppings.

He turned down a spiral of stairs. I turned up it. The attics lurked at the top. A moment too late I heard a sound from on high. The same cheeping, silken sound of the royal park treetops. That same susurration.

I whipped round to fling myself off a stair step, but tangled in my tail. And they were all over me, battering me about by the rush of their black wings. And again that dire smell of mildew and undigested insect. Webby hands seized me under my arms and once more I was rising through dark air. My hands and feet dangled.

Whoever they were—whatever—they were sure of their way. We swerved from attic to attic, skimming the slanting ceilings. They kept up a steady cheeping in both my ears, but I heard their separate hearts.

PALACE ATTICS ARE crowded places. The footmen sleep in some of them, and dress in pairs.

In others, aged boot boys and clock winders live out their lives, slumped at the feet of their bunks. And in certain attics, where no human foot falls and long-forgotten luggage stands in stacks, live the bats.

Bats! Of course—the webby hands, the silken wings. The row on row of chattering teeth. Bats! I'd been in their terrible power as soon as Peg had flicked me out of his ear. They'd monitored my entire Yeomouse career from their cheeping treetops. Though they hang upside-down, they miss nothing.

Now we were in their lair at last, this batty attic. Circling, they dropped me like a parcel on a floor thick with beetle shells, and worse.

I sprawled.

The pair of them who had twice mouse-napped me settled on the rafter just above. With their spooky, spokey fingers, they drew their wings about themselves and looked down, keeping their red eyes on me.

Mine adjusted to the awful dark. There were bats everywhere, folded like umbrellas hung from rafters and luggage straps.

A major infestation. Many more than twelve. Many. It was a bat barracks, a . . . battery. They seemed to sleep in shifts. My two were crouching watch over me.

And up there on the top rafter in one faint golden glimmer was my Yeomouse uniform hanging from a splinter in a pinpoint of light.

"My uniform!" I cried out.

The bats gazed down at me. They were nearly cheek to cheek with their chins propped on their ghastly gathered hands. Being bats, they had mustaches. Hideous, really.

"You von't be needing your univorm," said one of them.

Of course they'd be foreign, being bats. Romanian. Transylvanian. Something.

"No," said the other one, "de last thing you vill need is dat univorm."

So all was lost. Once more I glimpsed a scene that was surely only moments ahead: the pair of them picking my bones clean in the privacy of these bat barracks. I remembered my sword plunged somewhere in the distant palace gardens and gave myself up for lost, just short of my goal. All my struggle, and no success. I was a goner. Rats will eat anything smaller than they are. Bats will eat anything at all. Bats can live on mosquitoes, and if you can live on mosquitoes, you'll eat anything.

They are omnivores, as any schoolboy knows. The word came straight from my old headmaster's vocabulary list. I thought fondly of my brief past, even of school, as my future seemed to grow shorter than I was. I wondered if tasting of strawberry would work *for* me or against me.

With that very thought, a small, hunched figure bustled around from the far side of a steamer trunk covered with ancient labels.

She seemed robed. But then, bats' wings are joined to their hands in rather an odd arrangement. When they aren't in flight, they all seem to be wearing robes. Shrouds, really. Under her wings this bat wore a starchy white apron. Between her ears a crisp cap. She was no bigger than I, but all business. Some sort of housekeeper, if you can imagine a bat in that position. She sized me up in an instant.

"Nobody said 'e'd be pink with black bits!"

Her hands seemed to be on her hips. You couldn't really see, for the wings. "'Ere, you two!" She squinted up to the rafter with my bats on it. "Wot's the meaning of this? You were to deliver 'im in good condition. Rules is rules."

Silence came from up there. Then one of them spoke. "Vee drooped him into a pole of bunch."

"A wot?" Her cheeping voice had a real edge to it. Not foreign, but common as a cat.

"A bowl of punch," I said.

"Honestly." Her red eyes rolled. "You can't get

'elp nowadays. Nobody wants to work, and that pair 'aven't a brain between them. Come with me. I 'ave some 'ot water ready."

"Am I to be boiled and eaten?" All the fight had gone out of me.

Bats are weak-eyed. She squinted at me. "Boiled and eaten? Not that I know of. But that pink is not a good color on you. You're to be washed and outfitted. Step lively and show a pair of 'eels, or I'll 'ave orf your 'ead myself."

The far side of the steamer trunk was busy with bats. The crumbly floor was black with them. Some in starchy caps with their wings rolled up and hard at work. There was the odd bat valet in a striped waistcoat, smelling of leather soap and Brasso. There was even a bat barber, as I was to learn. This end of the attic seemed to be a sort of bat servants' hall. The world is an unexpected place, but then, bats need their support staff like anybody else.

When the bat housekeeper marched me into

their midst, needlebats looked up from their mending. Bat laundresses lifted their streaming faces from copper boilers.

And they all had something to cheep. "Vat a peculiar color." And "Surely not his natural shade." And "Vat are dem black bits?" And, of course, "Is he not yet full-grown or just short?"

A pair of small laundresses stepped up with pails of soapy water to dash over me. Then they set about me with a pair of bristly brushes till I was back to my natural gray, slumping in a pool of pink with floating black bits.

"Posture," a laundress hissed into my ear before they withdrew.

And in, say, twelve minutes more I stood in front of a human lady's mirror, gone missing from her reticule. It leaned against the steamer trunk. If you're missing a pocket mirror, a bat probably has it unless a magpie took it off you. Very vain, magpies and bats, though heaven knows why.

As I wasn't so slick now, it had taken several bat valets to get me into my new uniform, using buttonhooks. It fit like a footman's glove. And when I saw myself in the mirror, I took my breath away. It was by far the best uniform ever seen. Blinding white against my natural gray with row on row of gold buttons. There was plenty of room up top for a chest I did not have and for medals I had not won. Epaulets, gold-fringed, gave me shoulders. A high braided collar made much of my neck and even offered up a bit of chin.

And a sword strapped on. Only for show, of course, but gold. And I had a hat, to be held in the crook of my arm. A white tropical hat exploding with pinfeathers.

The uniform of the Yeomice of the Guard wasn't a patch on this one. If Princess Ena had only seen me as I was now, she'd have fallen off her pony twice.

At the last moment a bat barber had stepped up to give my whiskers a light trim and to even

When I saw myself in the mirror, I took my breath away.

up my ears somewhat. My head was swollen and awhirl. I was either about to become the Head Doormouse at the Ritz Hotel or a case of mistaken identity. I only hoped they wouldn't take away this uniform too soon. By now I'd quite forgotten about being boiled and eaten.

Bats flocked, to admire my finery and to catch glimpses of themselves in the looking glass. I hung in a great fog of their mildew and undigested insects, wondering how long this could last.

They had done me up for some grand function, even an appearance at court.

Court?

Could it be? "I say," I said to the clustering bats, "this is surely court attire. Am I to have an audience with Her Mouse Majesty, the Queen of the Mice?" It seemed too good to be true, and I wondered if Queen Victoria had put in a word for me.

But all was silence around me. Then a great cheep welled up. My mousenappers swooped in from their rafter and ran riot over our heads, cheeping in horror and warning. Every bat was at sixes and sevens.

What had I said?

The bat housekeeper took her hand from her mouth to say, "Never mention the Personage you just mentioned. She stands at the top of the Great Truth and Central Secret of the British Empire! Some things is too Mighty and Mysterious to bandy about. Besides, it raises too many questions.

"Blimey, 'oo doesn't know that?" she added. "Were you born in a barn?"

How embarrassing, I thought. But then a voice echoed through the batty attics:

*"His Excellency the Bat Chancellor and Air Marshal vill see him now."*

I jumped. What next? Webby hands set about me. I glittered one last moment in the mirror. "But who *is* he?" I called out to the housekeeper.

"'Oo indeed!" she replied. "Only the chief advisor of She Who Carn't Be Spoken of Aloud, that's 'oo! Mice can't make a move without bats. 'Oo doesn't know that? Orf you go. Rules is rules."

At least I was dressed for the occasion. I looked down me, and above a button I saw tiny stitchery in gold thread. An *A* and an *M* with a small flourish.

*A.M.* Aunt Marigold. She'd made this uniform. Every tuck taken was hers. I recalled how she used to snatch me up by the tail to tell me of my shortcomings. And so my heart and eyes were full as I was led off to the Bat Chancellor and Air Marshal for reasons too mysterious to mention. And because mice can't make a move without bats.

# CHAPTER TWELVE

# Fate Unfolds

**A**N OLD PLUSH curtain hung from a rafter. Worrisome hands swept it aside, and I was led up. In the gloom beyond, dozens and dozens and dozens of bats stood row on row. They looked like judge and jury to me. Black silk wings wrapped tight as cigars. On their heads were strange, out-of-date hats with tassels hanging down. Medals for unknown battles swung from their hollow chests. Some were withered by time. Some were so scary, you wondered if they could see themselves in mirrors.

The chamber burned red from their eyes. And the smell could knock you down.

Bats, bats on every side. Poking fingers thrust me forward across the murmuring attic. Like the cheeping treetops, they chanted:

> *From burrows deep*
> *To manger hay,*
> *We were never far away.*

And:

> *From horse's ear*
> *To Yeomouse red,*
> *You were never far ahead.*

It was all eerie in the extreme. Dead ahead now, a figure hulked over us on a Twinings Tea caddy. A crabbed and crouching shape, dusty against the dimness. His eyes were embers behind his smoked spectacles. His clutching fingers were like the spindly spokes of a broken umbrella. He pointed one of those dismal digits down at me.

My feathered headgear nearly took flight out of the crook of my arm. My knees were a pair of jellies.

"Mouse Minor!" he cheeped in a voice like a rusty hinge.

No. How could it be? But it was. Only my uniform held me together. Only my tail kept me upright.

Here looming over me was the ancient headmaster of the Royal Mews Mouse Academy. It was B. Chiroptera, M.A., our old teacher. Suddenly I was back in the schoolroom where I'd begun. My knuckles remembered, and throbbed. Even the smell was familiar.

It is unnatural to see any teacher outside school. But this was stranger still. He was a bat?

Of course he was. Why hadn't we seen? That grim gown wrapped round him had been his furled and musty wings. Those rows and rows of chattering teeth. The dim rubies of his eyes behind the smoked lenses. Those naps he stole through the day because bats are nocturnal.

Nocturnal! Another word from his endless vocabulary list. We scholars had thought he was merely old and crazy. He was, of course, but he was a bat into the bargain.

As well as Bat Chancellor and Air Marshal, whatever that might mean. A double life? A secret agent? You never know the full truth about a teacher. And he was everywhere I turned, practically in two places at once. But then, bats can fly. Very worrying.

"What a merry chase you have led us from a schoolroom where you benefited from my teaching *and* protection," he wheezed, shaking his scaly old head.

"All the right sort of schools are bat-run, of course, from burrow to belfry," he said, off on a tangent as usual. "How much the world has to learn from us. Yes, I think you'll find that all the best teachers are old bats."

He sighed in admiration of bats everywhere, especially himself, and plunged on: "If only there were time in this crowded day, I could expand upon the importance of bats. We are a quarter of all mammals and the only mammals who fly. And so we are both faculty and air force, as you have reason to know. And an air force is a thing humans will never have! Where are their wings?"

He was droning on as he does, and drifting far off the point. A bat or two near me yawned.

But then he remembered himself and wrapped his robes. "And now your flight has ended, Sir! You vanished just when you were most needed. But scamper all you will, you cannot escape your fate. And justice will be done!"

Bats circled me silkily, chanting:

> *He can run, but he can't hide,*
> *Comes soon the moment to decide.*

Decide? Decide what? *Oh wake me from this nightmare*, I squealed inside. But it was no nightmare. It was every bit as real as the rest of this story.

My knuckles throbbed and the collar tightened round my throat. They couldn't have my head off. This wasn't France. Still, they might easily throw me in irons and put me away till the next reign. With dungeon doors clanging in my head, I broke my silence. Squaring my gold-fringed shoulders, I squeaked up.

"It's unfair." I stamped a small foot.

The bats boggled and looked blank. "Unfair?"

The chancellor trained his smoky lenses on me. "In what regard, Sir?"

"I confess I ran away from school," I squeaked. "And at just the wrong time. If only I'd hung on till today, there'd have been a party for the jubilee, with cake. And yes, showing myself in school uniform to a human raises entirely too many questions. But I hardly think this calls for two mousenappings and a trial. Besides, you're not a jury of my peers. You're *bats.*"

I began rather to like the sound of my own squeak. "Have you nothing better to do than persecute the runtiest mouse in the Mews?" I shrank up a bit in the uniform, though it fit like a glove.

"Besides, I can't be blamed for anything because I'm nameless. And . . . Nameless is Blameless."

You could have heard a pin drop. Bats stared. "He thinks he's nameless," they murmured among themselves. Their tassels swayed. "And he takes us for a jury? What poppycock. We are Gentlebats in Waiting to His Excellency B. Chiroptera, Bat Chancellor to Her Unmentionable Majesty. Mice make the world go round, but they can't budge without bats." Etc. Then they began to chant:

> *Back, back through the mists of time*
> *Rodents have sat on their throne,*

*Whilst bats, the ideal courtiers,*
*Set the proper tone.*

It was annoying how bats in a bunch were apt to break into verse. As it happened, they thought they were bards. *And* they claimed mice can't rhyme. But old B. Chiroptera didn't like being interrupted. "You have a name, Sir!" he blared into my face. "Everybody has a name. Well, not field mice, but—"

"Then what *is* my name, Your . . . Excellency?"

"Why, Ludovic. Naturally."

"Ludovic?"

"Ludovic," all the bats agreed.

I'd waited all this time for a name, and it turned out to be Ludovic?

Old B. Chiroptera drew himself up to a higher hunch. "If only you had been listening in history class, you would have learned that the heir to the Mouse Monarchy is always named Ludovic. Right the way back to Ludovic the Confessor and Ludovic the Conqueror. 1066 and all that."

This was somewhat interesting, as history goes, though unclear. "I'm named for a Prince?"

"No, Your Royal Highness." My old teacher bowed his scaly head. "You *are* the Prince."

ALL THE BATS bowed, as you do, from the neck. And they were all bowing in my direction. Old Chiroptera himself was bowing. You cannot know the joy of seeing your old teacher bow before you.

But my breathing grew shallow. My knees began to buckle, like Prince Havarti coming down the comb. I looked behind myself to make sure they weren't bowing to somebody else.

In fact, a figure stood behind me, just beyond my question mark tail. Another mouse.

He was formally turned out as a Mouse Equerry, in morning clothes for Jubilee Day. A tailcoat over striped trousers, a silk top hat in the crook of his arm. A dogtooth violet in his

He too was bowing to me, Ian was.
"Your Royal Highness," he said.

buttonhole. Very smart, very aristocratic, right down to his claw-tips.

It was Ian.

Yeomouse Ian of the high-born Henslowes. Ian, who had managed the mousenapping that had led us both to this moment.

He too was bowing to me, Ian was. "Your Royal Highness," he said, from the neck as you . . .

The attic went darker, and tilted. I remember nothing more.

IN MY WHOLE body I have only two teaspoons of blood. It usually keeps quite busy. But the shock of learning who I was—and being named Ludovic—drained all the blood from my brain. The feathered helmet keeled out of my crooked arm. My knees went. Then my posture. Not even my question mark tail kept me upright. Crumpling, I fainted.

Embarrassing, but these things happen.

When I came to, I was lolling in a spectacles

case from somewhere, my tail and sword draped over the side. Ian, Mouse Equerry, was applying a cold compress to my forehead. He seemed to fade out, then fade in again. Sometimes there were three of him. But it takes no time at all to get used to being called Your Royal Highness.

"Your Royal Highness," Ian was saying, "I hope you didn't faint from hunger. There's nothing whatever to eat in these attics but mosquitoes. Stir-fried, but still . . ."

"No, thank you," I said, very mousy. I couldn't have kept a gnat down.

And even now the Gentlebats in Waiting were gathering themselves for another of their choral readings. There was really no stopping them:

*The child of a forbidden marriage,*
*Mews-bred and never seen,*
*For it never ever pays*
*To cross his grandmother, the Queen.*

This seemed to be me in a nutshell, though badly rhymed and with several important details left out.

Where to begin? I lolled there in the spectacles case, somewhere between the mouse I had been and the mouse I would be. Ian stood by, correct as ever. How much I admired the droop of his whiskers. But was he friend or foe? Royalty needs to know.

"Ian," I asked, "were you or were you not a Yeomouse of the Guard? A real one?"

He coughed quietly behind a hand. "I was a Yeomouse just for a day, Sir. Rather like yourself. Once you were discovered in their ranks after you'd gone missing from school, I was sent by the Bat Chancellor to . . . arrange for your removal."

I drew a veil in my mind over my so-called removal—being snatched up into the night air and dropping into a pole of bunch. It didn't bear thinking about. "Ian," I said, "have you a proper palace job, or are you a gentlemouse of leisure?"

"As I have told you, Sir, I am a younger son, and so I must make my way in the world. I have been in training to be Mouse Equerry to the heir to the Mouse Throne."

Oh, I thought. "And that would be me?"

"In fact it's meant to be Prince Bruno of the Havartis. The Queen of the Mice has had to look as far as Denmark for an heir. She does not know you exist. Your mother, the Princess Royal, dared marry for love. When she died at your birth, the Queen was told that you died too. It was too dangerous to tell her you lived. We try not to cross her."

"Ah yes, I've been told that my . . . grandmother lacks the human Queen Victoria's sunny disposition. In fact it was Queen Victoria herself who told me."

Ian boggled. The Bat Chancellor blinked. He

hovered nearby, a bit worried I might scamper down the nearest mousehole again, feathered hat and all.

"Yes, Ian. I am able to communicate with a human if I squeak up, at least with Queen Victoria. Do you suppose it's because I am half royal myself?"

"Very possibly," Ian said faintly. "Her Human Majesty granted you an audience?"

"Yes, not long after I'd given the Bat Air Force the slip and took that swan dive into the strawberry punch."

Old B. Chiroptera winced.

"She rather had to grant me an audience. I was in her saucer."

"If you say so, Sir," Ian said with quiet dignity. "And did you arrive by horse?"

"No, Ian. By then Peg would have been snug in the Mews and fast asleep. I arrived on a chambermaid's apron strings."

"Just as you say, Sir," Ian said.

Why am I so hard to believe? I always tell the truth.

But by then we were all realizing the jubilee morning was ticking away. Every moment took us nearer a first meeting with my grandmother, the Queen of the Mice. It was a lot to think about. You could hear my heart.

"I suppose I shall come as a great surprise to Her Majesty." I had staggered out of the spectacles case and stood swaying. Ian was giving my feathered hat a brush and handing it to me.

"Yes," he said sadly, "and Her Majesty hates surprises."

To speed me on my way, the bat bards broke into yet another of their verses:

> *Make way for the undersized Princeling—*
> *His very existence unknown—*
> *As he braves his way on Jubilee Day,*
> *Bound for the royal throne.*

Very annoying. And they weren't finished:

> *Onward he ventures, this scrap of a mouse,*
> *Approaching his crucial hour;*
> *Gird his small loins with our best advice:*
> *Never say no to power.*

Then out of nowhere webby hands seized me in steely grips and jerked me upward. Breeze rushed between my toes. The attic floor and Ian fell away below me. I could feel the beat of the bat pilots' separate hearts. Apparently I was traveling to my fate by air.

# CHAPTER THIRTEEN

# A Field of Gray

WHILE QUEEN VICTORIA was still at breakfast in her bedchamber that morning, her jubilee procession was already beginning to pass through the gold-tipped palace gates below.

You could hear the proud clatter of hoofs from wherever you happened to be. And the roar of the crowd.

At eleven the first guns fired their salute. How well I knew eleven from the ruler. At a quarter past it, Queen Victoria rolled out through the gates in a landau drawn by eight of the best

Windsor Greys with Peg in the lead position. High-stepping Peg, whose brasses blazed in the cloudless blue-sky day.

He led the way right across London through a sea of flags and crowds singing "God Save the Queen" to the steps of St. Paul's, where the world gave thanks for all the years of Queen Victoria's long reign.

In a queue of carriages behind came the royal children and grandchildren. Forty grandchildren. They waved back to the crowds and shook small Union Jacks.

I cannot say I saw this brave sight myself. But it is recorded for all history to come, as it was the first great event captured by the new moving-picture camera. Pictures that move! Whatever next?

WHEN DISTANCE HAD swallowed the procession, silence fell on Buckingham Palace. All the help melted away like the dew on the morning. The Pages of the Presence and the Pages of the Back Stairs. The Body Linen Laundresses and the Bedchamber Women. The Fire Lighters and Footmen, the Butlers and Under Butlers. The lot. Human servants work very little in the absence of their masters. They are often in the kitchens, swilling champagne. When the cat's away . . . if you'll excuse the expression.

For a single moment the great palace was like a picture of itself, framed in quiet. Nothing moved until the next moment when the palace flickered to life again.

Fur stirred. Fur the same gray as the shadows. Floral arrangements grew ears. From somewhere a handkerchief skirt whisked across parquet. And suddenly the palace burst into new being. Every palace—every house—gets busier when the humans are away. Every time a human walks out of a room, something with more feet walks in.

Long velvet curtains swayed, and mice

dropped down. Antimacassars moved, and mouse snouts thrust up through the cutwork. From across gilt frames in the Picture Gallery, mice crept in long lines, and from every crack in the plaster. Tails added to the fringe on the upholstery. Chandeliers tinkled with us. We were everywhere. Tapestries rippled mysteriously.

Bats may have us all outnumbered, but the mice of Buckingham Palace far outnumber the palace humans. And we naturally make better use of the space.

As a rule, the greatest rodent events must take place in the darkest watches of the night. But on Diamond Jubilee Day let the sun shine upon us. Let great shafts of light fall across the grand clutter and marble paving of these royal rooms, and us!

And so we used every cranny and crevice and anteroom. We regrouped in butlers' pantries and fanned out. We swarmed out of every royal water closet, flushed with excitement. A very high society mouse wedding was under way before the hearth in Princess Louise's suite. Mouse mites were being christened at the foot of the font in the Royal Chapel.

But the real and royal reason for our day lay yet ahead. In fact Queen Victoria's entire Diamond Jubilee might have been arranged for a different Monarch altogether, and her alone.

The palace clocks were ticking toward twelve when Her Unmentionable Majesty the Queen of the Mice would receive the foreign delegations in a special Jubilee Court. There was loose talk of a surprise announcement. After all, the Queen of the Mice was getting on. Power would pass. But to whom? Rodent rumors ran riot.

And so as the clocks nudged noon, the best-born mice from across Europe made their way to the Throne Room, where prisms drip against gold, and power pulsates.

The Throne Room dwarfs humans, let alone

mice. But the floor was a field of gray, aglitter with mouse medals and tiny tiaras. How proud they were to be admitted to the Great Sovereign Secrecy of the Court. For after all, if the Queen of the Mice were common knowledge, it would raise too many questions, some of them in Parliament.

And so every regal snout from here to Greece turned to the empty dais below Victoria's throne, waiting for what came next. Commoner mice clung to the edges of the crowd: regular, everyday mice who keep the palace and the Mews and the world ticking over. More useful than royals, really.

It was a moment in history that did not lack witnesses, who told and retold the tale long after.

The choristers were the first through that mousehole behind the throne. Mice boys from the Palace Choir School that keeps within the walls of the Music Room and inside the grand piano. In they filed, jostling and pulling one another's tail, as you do. They formed into two lines to scamper up the rear legs of the throne. Not an easy job in their robes with big pussycat bows, if you'll excuse the expression, under their little pointed chins.

They assembled, sopranos all, up there on the seat of the throne, a choir loft now. Then they burst into what was our Mouse National Anthem before the humans got to it:

> *"Land of hope and glory,*
> *Mother of the Cheese!"*

the choristers sang. Being boys, they were always hungry.

Mice of all dynasties stood stiffly to attention, right back to the Bulgarians at the rear of the room. How long they'd rehearsed those bows, those curtsies.

The choristers' last squeaks still hung in the air when through the mousehole trooped the Yeomice of the Guard, all in scarlet with the streamers streaming from their mushroom caps. Clanking with cutlery, they swarmed into a massive force around the four claw feet of the throne.

In command was the Captain of the Yeomice, more imposing off his chipmunk than on it. How perfect his posture, his body beneath the gold fringe all muscle like a hummingbird. His back-flung shoulders massive in mouse terms.

The room grew restless, sensing the approaching presence of the Queen. Tails flailed. You could have cut the tension with a cheese knife. But first, here came her faithful retainers, the bats, in a haze of undigested insects. The Bat Chancellor and Air Marshal, old B. Chiroptera, lurched along in the lead.

Nothing very festive about bats, of course. Not a handsome species. They hardly have profiles. Better behind the scenes. Far better. But they too must have their Jubilee Day in the focus of fame. Room on the dais was made for them, black against the scarlet of the Yeomice.

There followed the ladies-in-waiting, and so the Queen herself was not more than a whisker away. Her Dames of the Bedchamber, Rodentesses of the Royal Personage, Mice Maids of Honor were all in full court feather. Their skirts were so enormous, they had to be thrust from behind by many hands through the mousehole.

The dais sparkled with the diamond chips in their ears and far down their furry fronts. How wasp their waists, though mice don't really have waists. They bore floral tributes to their Queen, scattering petals, and arranged themselves picturesquely, blotting out the bats. You cannot beat the English for pageantry. And mice we may be, but we are English first. All Europe was agog.

Now the great moment was at hand. Mouse pages in powdered wigs unrolled a long hair ribbon to serve as red carpet, from the mousehole to the very front of the dais. Yeomice presented arms. Bats bowed. Ladies-in-waiting fell to the floor in their curtsies. Above, the choristers were all eyes, hungry for their first glimpse of her, the Mother of their Cheese.

Then she was there, suddenly visible, thrust by many hands from the darkness of mystery to the glare of the Throne Room. She was no longer slender, and her skirts were half a ruler wide. When these skirts settled around her, they were butterfly wings sewn in an intricate pattern. I knew that needlework. I knew the nets that had trapped the butterflies.

The Queen of the Mice shimmered in every color as she advanced along the red carpet. Though as a rule she wore only deepest black, in mourning for her daughter, the Princess Royal. But then Her Human Majesty Queen Victoria had herself today left off the black mourning for her late husband. Perhaps this pair of queens had decided it between themselves.

Mice are not known for their necks, but the Queen was roped with seed pearls from chin to knee. Her crown was a diamond ring similar to one that had gone missing from Princess Alexandra's jewel case some while back, though a reward was still offered for its recovery. The Queen came forth as if on a set of small wheels. Her skirts fluttered like flight.

Now she stood before the throne, arranging shawls as fine as spiderweb around her gray shoulders. She looked out over all the Europe that counted. And she did not appear happy to see them, though the room was practically on its knees and bowing from the neck as you do.

"Bela!" the Queen of the Mice cried out.

Bela?

"Where is he? We want Bela!"

And from the bats beyond her, the Bat Chancellor loomed forth. *Bela?* The *B* in B. Chiroptera was for *Bela?*

"Your Majesty?" he inquired into her jeweled ear.

"Time is running very short, Bela," she said in a stage whisper. "The Others will soon be back." She meant the human royals. For mice, time is always running out. We are all rather here today—

"We haven't the time for proper presentations," snapped the Queen. "Run the foreign delegations past us. And let us take them at the gallop." She sighed. "So many of them, so few of ourself."

And so the foreigners came, waved on by the Bat Chancellor. They flowed past the dais in a jiggle of quick bows and sudden curtsies. The Germans first, with small spikes on the tops of their helmets and tiny jackboots. And what a lot of them: every living Liederkranz and all the Limburgers. An unbearable number of barons and countless countesses.

The Belgians followed in a great mob. And hard on their heels the Spanish, their claws clicking like castanets across the marble. Then the Russians in all their barbaric splendor.

Romanov rodents in caterpillar-fur caps. Even one of the Gorgonzola princes from Italy, looking very blue-veined.

Then here came the Danes.

The Queen had been frozen in dignity and disapproval. Now she thawed. Her gaze skipped over several Danish princesses and fell upon Bruno, Prince Havarti. He was packed into his court clothes. A ribbon rattling with medals strained across his front. His breeches ballooned behind.

With the smallest of gestures, the Queen of the Mice summoned him forth, while the world craned their necks to see.

It took Prince Bruno two tries and a boost from behind to make it up onto the dais. It had been hard enough for him to get down the comb at the wreath-laying ceremony. But at last he was before the Queen. Damply, he bowed as low as he could.

Rumor had reached the farthest end of the room—right back to the Bulgarians—that the Queen of the Mice might make a startling and historic announcement. But, wait—she's speaking now:

"We stand before you, a childless widow, who must selflessly think of the future of the Throne. And so we have searched every branch and twig of the family tree for our successor."

Every royal in the room was her cousin, one way or another, a twig on her tree. But she had made her choice.

"Indeed we have had to look to distant Denmark to find our perfect heir, and here he is: a younger son, related to us on both sides, and with no ideas of his own. Ideal!" She pointed out Prince Bruno, though he hulked over her.

The Prince stared blankly out over the crowd, bulbous and beardless. You couldn't see his feet. He looked hungry.

"And so we take the opportunity of this Jubilee Court," proclaimed the Queen, "to announce that our heir and Crown Prince is to be—"

"Our grandson," old Bela Chiroptera broke in. "Or rather your grandson, Your Majesty."

The Queen froze, then drew back. She sent a look like a death ray at old Bela. A question hung over her head: Had he gone completely batty?

It was quite true she didn't like surprises. Thunder rolled across her face. Her snout quivered, and she showed teeth.

"We have no grandson, Bela," she said in a dangerous voice.

"In fact you have, Your Majesty," old B. Chiroptera wheezed before the listening room. He was glad of the witnesses. "I have seen to his education personally in one of the top five schools of—"

"Bela!" barked the Queen, "have you dared go behind our back to meddle in our personal family affairs? Have you *plotted?*"

"Your Majesty, I have." He wrapped his shroudly wings tight around him. "What use is a

Royal Court without intrigue? And all in a good cause."

The eyes of the Mouse Queen narrowed. "In Hungary there'd be a stake through your heart by now, Bela," she remarked. "And you may thank your lucky stars that we are not French. If only we were, you would be looking high and low for your head."

"Your Majesty," he murmured, bowing his.

"Conspiracy! That's what this is, Bela, and we will not have it!" The old Bat Chancellor flinched. "If we have a grandson, produce him!"

The Queen of the Mice towered with rage. The room held its breath. Not a tiara tinkled. Into this silence old B. Chiroptera raised a hand from his shroud and snapped his dismal digits.

And I flew down from the nearest chandelier, hung by the underarms from a pair of bats wearing miniature goggles and small silk scarves, fringed, around their necks. They dropped me directly before the Queen. I nearly tangled in my

I flew down from the nearest chandelier.

sword, but did a little dance and lit on my feet. The bat pilots swerved away, their scarves flapping, their black wings churning the air.

I know. I know. Things were happening too fast for me too. But that's the way it was, with plenty of witnesses. I managed to whip off my feathered hat and bow from the neck. "Your Majesty," I squeaked.

Up close, she was a real rodent, Her Mystical Majesty was. She dyed her whiskers. You could tell. But of course my heart was in my mouth. I'd never looked such power in the face. Her lips peeled back from her teeth in a worrying way. Only my tail kept me upright.

"Grandmother," I said, taking the plunge.

# A Hard Mouse to Convince

THE VERY DIAMOND in the Queen's crown flashed a warning. She was taller than I. Who isn't? Looking far down her snout, she spoke in a low and worrisome voice. All Europe leaned nearer to hear:

"You dare call me Grandmother? I have never been called . . ." Her voice wavered. She glanced away. "Imposter!" she snapped. "We have no grandson!" She looked far down me now. "And if we did have a grandson, he'd be bigger. Or are you not yet full-grown?"

I sighed.

Then out of the crowd rang a voice: "Oh yes, Your Majesty. That's your grandson right there, small as life!" How well I knew that voice. My eyes grew misty.

The crowds parted, and two figures approached. Ian was there, top hat in one arm and on his other arm a mouse of mature years in a starchy apron. Her whiskers were grizzled bristles, over the scissor teeth. She had never been a beauty.

It was Aunt Marigold. Aunt Marigold, *here*. Though she was no stranger to the palace, with her mending basket, going about her business.

Ian handed her nearer the dais. The Queen pointed a finger down at Aunty. "You too, Marigold?" she intoned in a voice like a bad dream. Aunt Marigold seemed to remove a bit of loose thread from her mouth. A pin glittered. "Yes, Your Majesty."

The Queen glowered. "An overdressed, not-quite-life-sized imposter has been dropped from the chandelier as if from heaven at our feet, and we are to accept him as our grandson! How many kinds of a fool do you take us for? And what part in this miserable business do *you* play, Marigold? Remember, time and my temper grow short."

The pin worked round in Aunt Marigold's mouth. Then she spoke. "I myself removed your grandson from his dying mother, before his eyes were open. They're barely open now. I brought him home to the Mews in my mending basket and incubated him personally—baked him like tea cake. I fed him on goats' milk a drop at a time, hand-reared him, and there he stands before you! Though he was touch-and-go right from the start."

Only then did Aunt Marigold remember to curtsy. She held out her apron in both hands and dropped a small one.

The Queen reflected. She was a hard mouse to convince, and there was nothing sunny about her disposition. She looked down upon her dazzling butterfly skirts. "You should have kept to your needlework, Marigold. Now you are apt to find yourself sewing mail bags in one of our damper prisons.

"As for you, Ian Henslowe, your career at this court is concluded."

Ian bowed, as for the last time, from the neck, as you do.

Now it was my turn. She looked just over my head and gave her dyed whiskers a twitch. Into the awful silence drifted the strains of distant music. It was a marching band of humans playing "Rule Britannia." The jubilee parade was returning to the palace. Queen Victoria and all her court and her forty grandchildren.

Time was running out. For mice it always is.

And so the Queen was to make short work of me. "You are banished from this court," she said briefly. "Whoever you are, be gone."

Never say no to power, but I had not particularly liked how the Queen had spoken to my aunt Marigold. And my mind was already scampering ahead, which was not like me. "Your Majesty," I inquired, "may I keep the uniform?"

She boggled. "The uniform?"

"Yes, Your Majesty. It's Aunty's best work. And it would come in handy if I found a job as doormouse at the Ritz Hotel. I understand that the hotel is infested with us. And once I am employed, I shall send for Aunt Marigold. We will not trouble you further."

I can't tell you where this plan came from. It was looking ahead, and I never had: And where did I get the nerve to blurt it out? It must have been the royal half of me, squeaking up.

As nobody talks back to her, the Queen

looked somewhat at sea. "We do not concern ourselves with such matters. Uniforms are bat business. Withdraw. Go."

What choice did I have? Besides, the Others were practically at the palace gates now. Still, in that moment I managed to make my worst mistake yet. You see it coming, don't you? I'd meant to drop down from the dais, to Aunt Marigold and Ian. And I was hurrying, never a good plan.

I turned my back on royalty.

Yes. What was I thinking?

This sent the room into uproar. Even the chandeliers cheeped. You never turn tail on your Sovereign Queen. Europe didn't know where to look. Greeks gasped. Croats cried out.

I was almost in the air when the Queen called out behind me: "Halt!" I scrabbled at the dais's edge.

To all our Royal Rulers we are spineless, but I was showing mine. Well-tailored, but still . . .

"Revolve," the Queen commanded. Carefully,

I turned back to her. The doors of damp prisons clanged in my head.

Somehow my feathered hat was still in the crook of my arm. I slumped before my Sovereign. My posture was completely gone.

"Your tail," she said. "It falls in the form of a question mark."

It was too late to tuck it away. Besides, it had a mind of its own. I was very nearly at the end of my string.

"Why do you suppose you have a question mark tail?" The Queen's eyebrows were high, though she hardly had any.

"Is it because I am of a curious and questing nature, Your Majesty?"

"We shouldn't think so," she said. "But every male mouse of the Royal Line has a question mark tail, right back to 1066 and all that. It is an inherited trait and comes with the job."

The human band was blaring "Rule Britannia" in the very forecourt of the palace.

"We may have been hasty," said the Queen of the Mice. "Tails never lie. It would appear that you are our grandson."

I DROPPED TO one knee before her, as I supposed you do. My tail asked a large and looping question across the red carpet. The Queen reached down and touched my forehead with a royal finger.

"Arise, Prince Ludovic," she proclaimed.

The room erupted. The humans were practically upon us. But at the last moment—the eleventh hour—the Successor to the Mouse Queen's Throne had been revealed. Everyone here had heard it first. Applause broke out, though mice applause is not deafening.

Throughout the entire proceedings you could hear Prince Bruno's breathing. He hulked beside us, his tail any old way, his feet invisible.

Looking around sadly at all this vanishing splendor, he asked in quite a whiny way, "Does this mean I have to go back to Copenhagen?"

Everybody was ready to bolt now. The ladies-in-waiting began to dither. The bats were about to unfurl and fly. The Yeomice of the Guard were considering retreat. The choristers had scrambled off the throne already. In mere moments Her Human Majesty, Queen Victoria would be settling onto this throne. Though it took an act of Parliament to get her out of her carriage and a block and tackle to drop her on her dais.

By then all the Best Mice of Europe would have melted like the dew on the morning, into the walls, beneath the floors, through every crevice and crack. But only a whisker away, as we always are.

Time ticked away, but I had a final question. The Queen, my grandmother, read it in my eyes, or perhaps my tail. You can imagine what it was.

"You will want to know about your father."

The Queen's hands worked before her. "He was not royal, and he was not our choice. Two strikes against him. Big ones. Our Daughter, your mother, had married for love, not duty. And that we could not have."

The Queen's eyes were glistening now and about to brim.

She looked out over her disappearing audience. Her Jubilee Court was drawing to a close. The Throne Room floor was no longer a solid gray with tiaras and tails. Patches of blank marble were appearing. The chandeliers were making final cheeps.

"But your father is of good family," the Queen said. "The Stiltons, with a proud history of service to Mousedom and the Crown. There were Stiltons in the Crimean War. A Stilton rode in the saddlebag for the Charge of the Light Brigade, we believe."

"And where shall I find my father?" I asked, knowing now what a big world it is.

"Beside you," said the Queen of the Mice.

I went blank, then I looked up, and my heart turned over. I had last seen him laying a wreath on a grave in the mysterious and mournful graveyard at the far end of the Palace Gardens. My mother's grave.

Now he had stepped up beside me, summoned by my grandmother. He was more imposing off his chipmunk than on it. He towered over me, all muscle like a humming-bird beneath his gold-fringed uniform. For my father was the Captain of the Yeomice of the Guard.

My heart sang, and my posture returned. He looked down at me in wonder, for I was as sudden a son as he was a sudden father.

It was important that I get this first bit right. And so I drew myself up as far as I would go. Then I gave him a smart salute, my spindly fingers splayed flat against my forehead.

He towered over me, all muscle like a hummingbird
beneath his gold-fringed uniform.

Smiling, he returned the salute.

Then he bent down and opened his arms, and I scampered into them.

# CHAPTER FIFTEEN

# Ludovic the 237th

ALL'S WELL THAT ends well, as some mouse surely said first.

But there is more than you'd think to being the future Mouse Monarch. More than a quick tap on the forehead and an "Arise, Prince Ludovic." Far more.

I first have to be made Rodent of Wales, and there will be a ceremony of Investiture. The Yeomice of the Guard band will play, and the choristers of the Palace Choir School will sing. A cheese board is planned. I hope you can come.

Aunt Marigold is at work on my outfit for this occasion. Something without pinfeathers in quiet good taste with grosgrain waistcoat. Rather in Ian's style, with a tailcoat: two tails plus my own. And a shiny top hat for the crook of my royal arm.

I'd hoped Aunt Marigold would come to live with Grandmother and me in Buckingham Palace. That's the best of living in a palace. There's always room for one more. Though I can't reveal precisely which walls we live within. Never let too much light in upon the Mystery of Majesty.

We could have made Aunt Marigold very comfortable, but she wouldn't hear of it. Very set in her ways is Aunty and wouldn't budge from her burrow. But then she *is* Head Needlemouse of the Mews, and you can't go higher in her world, that world that smells of horse and what horses leave behind.

Much the same is true for my father, the Captain of the Yeomice of the Guard. I could put his name up for a title, perhaps a Baron or even an Earl. Maybe a Duke if I could get it past Grandmother. After all, he will be a King's father one day.

But he has said no thank you, being proud of his rank as captain. Captains are more useful than Dukes anyway.

There are limits to a Crown Prince's power. I cannot pass out titles or anything else without going through the bat courtiers. Bats! And now that I am no longer scholar of the Royal Mews Mouse Academy, my old headmaster has returned to his post as full-time Bat Chancellor and Air Marshal. He is everywhere I turn.

But the great thing about being a Prince is having a Mouse Equerry, and I chose Ian. Everybody should have one. An equerry is a chum who always agrees with you, isn't he, Ian?

An equerry is a chum who always agrees with you, isn't he, Ian?

"Just as you say, Your Highness," says Ian.

Right now we're busy about our plans for the Rodent of Wales Investiture. It's meant to be the biggest event since Queen Victoria's Diamond Jubilee. On the guest list are my old schoolmates Trevor and Fitzherbert—the Four Fists. How surprised they will be by a Royal Command. But I am all for letting bygones be bygones, and I want to see them bow, from the neck, as you do.

And so the future unfurls, though we are in no hurry to see the end of Grandmother's reign. Long Live the Queen of the Mice. May she live for months and months to come.

But one day I shall be on the throne, and Ian reminds me that I will be Ludovic the 237th. So there have been a great many more than twelve Ludovics before me.

"I shan't make much of a showing," I say to Ian, "being small."

But he says, "Never mind, Sir. The crown will make you just as tall as you will need to be. It's what crowns are for." Ian always says the right thing.

It will be a very modern reign, the reign of Ludovic the 237th.

Flight is the way forward, so we mean to make great advances in our Royal Air Force, for patrolling our perimeters and ceremonial fly-overs. It will keep the bats busy, and it's better to keep them occupied or they are apt to burst into bad verse, teach school, or hang about in attics upside-down.

As for the pictures that move and the moving-picture camera that captured Queen Victoria's jubilee parade, this too shows promise. Watching Queen Victoria over and over will grow tiring, but why not a moving picture that features a mouse?

I know. I know. But it could happen.

A Royal Reign raises such issues—the future of flight, the flicker of film, and more. And do not expect to find all your answers in the first asking. But I have a history of looking for answers:

Who am I?

And who am I to be?

You may have wondered much the same about yourself.

So why wouldn't every one of our tales end with a question mark?

# About the Author

**D**ESCRIBED BY *The Washington Post* as "America's best living author for young adults," Richard Peck is the first children's book writer ever to have been awarded a National Humanities Medal. His extensive list of honors includes the Newbery Medal (for *A Year Down Yonder*), a Newbery Honor (for *A Long Way from Chicago*), the Edgar Award (for *Are You in the House Alone?*), the Scott O'Dell Award (for *The River Between Us*), the Christopher Medal (for *The Teacher's Funeral*), and the Margaret A. Edwards Award for lifetime achievement in young adult literature. He has twice been a finalist for the National Book Award. Mr. Peck lives in New York City.